THE BORDER

16 September

I do not know what to do about Hans' *affaire*, which continues, he maintains, only as friendship. The pain of it puzzles my head.

— Why didn't you tell me? I asked

— I didn't want it to spoil our love, he said. I could only gaze at him with incredulity.

— It's over, he said: I promise you.

— Really? I wanted to believe him. There was enough in the newspaper to frighten us into closeness again.

— Look at what has been happening in Vienna! They have old women mopping up streets. And such delight in looting and rape. Always rape.

— He sighed. But I could tell the shadow that crossed his face was from another threat.

— Have you arranged to see her again? I asked him, evenly.

— See who?

I knew he understood, and shrugged. So that he was forced to reply.

— Yes. Listen. Trust me. Will you trust me?

I didn't see what sense it made but I nodded.

By the same author

THE BORDER

Elaine Feinstein

Methuen

A Methuen Paperback

THE BORDER

First published in Great Britain 1984
by Hutchinson & Co (Publishers) Ltd
Copyright © 1984 Elaine Feinstein
This edition published 1985
by Methuen London Ltd
11 New Fetter Lane, London EC4P 4EE
Reproduced, printed and bound in Great Britain by
Hazell Watson & Viney Limited,
Member of the BPCC Group,
Aylesbury, Bucks

British Library Cataloguing in Publication Data

Feinstein, Elaine
    The border.
    I. Title
    823'.914[F]   PR6056.E38

    ISBN 0-413-57550-0

For Ruth Padel

WALTER BENJAMIN, born Berlin 1892, died Port Bou 1940. German-Jewish essayist of genius. Major work includes criticism of Baudelaire, Karl Kraus and Franz Kafka. Posthumous admirers, such as Hannah Arendt and Gershom Scholem, have disagreed about the weight of mysticism and Marxism in his thought.

Part One
SYDNEY
9 September 1983

'All sorrows can be borne if you put them into a
story or tell a story about them'
  Isak Dinesen

– A glass of tea? Or maybe a little schnapps?

The old woman's hair was arranged carefully about her perfectly shaped skull like skeins of beige silk. As the boy hesitated, she chuckled, and rose briskly on her neat, stick legs to bring over two glasses and a bottle of cognac.

In profile she looks like an eagle, the boy thought. Eighty-three, was she?

In her turn, he was scrutinized critically.

– A handsome young man. Such a lot of black curly hair. And good, narrow hips.

The boy marvelled at the way she had enclosed herself in a piece of Central Europe, as if she had conjured the walnut chest, inlaid tables, and curving velvet button-back chairs into place; or perhaps transported them with infinite care, to be reassembled in Australia, like the wooden house of the first Governor General in Melbourne. When she put a porcelain plate before him, with a plain yellow cake upon it, the aroma of nutmeg and cinnamon rose to his memory as if he had spent his own childhood in Vienna or Budapest.

Which he had not.

She seemed to guess his thoughts, although hardly answering their direction.

– A pity Frederick married so very *Californian* a wife. It has kept us apart, I think. What a fortune to have grandsons, at least, who resemble the child he was. Now. Tell me about yourself. Saul, isn't it? And you are a historian.

– At Oxford.

– Good. England is not much admired here, but I know

better. Is Hans' work read in England now? Is he remembered? He is translated in America, I know; but it would have mattered more to him to be read in London and Paris.

– I have read him in German, said the boy.

Her eyebrows rose.

– And do you find him good? I cannot read his poetry you know. It is a kind of blindness. Music, yes. Some paintings. But not poetry.

She patted his hand, as he sipped his cognac; and he smiled. An easy, lazy smile that lit his grey eyes and brought a sigh to the woman watching him.

– You live in another world now. Probably no better, but at least different. Well. It's a long haul from Europe. It was kind of you to come and see an old woman. I wonder what draws you. Oh yes, I know *you*, young man, more than you suppose. You are not a philanthropist. You are curious. Why?

She poured two more glasses of brandy, and her eyes grew black as she lay back comfortably.

– As a historian? Don't you find writers always have something of the vampire about them? Guiltless, naturally. But sucking the marrow bones of the rest of us none the less. Where else would they find the sweetness they need?

– You knew Walter Benjamin, said the young man, hesitantly.

The old woman put on her spectacles and sighed: Of course we knew Walter. A little. In that terrible French city we had gone to for refuge. How should we not know another one of the hunted? And Hans admired him.

– On the train, said the young man: South of Perpignan.

– Nobody travelled by train. It was not a practical plan, said the old woman sharply: In June, we broke down in Quercy, between the Dordogne and Lot. Hah. Where to begin our history of disastrous choices! For we had choices, there is no question in my mind as to that. The road forked so many times, and always we went up the wrong turning.

12

Supposing in 1937, for example. Supposing I had looked out of the window and said quite simply. Of course. It is obvious. It is what we both want.

She shifted restlessly in her chair.

– You must do whatever you like, I said instead, reasonably. So many choices women force upon men. Out of cowardice. Or perhaps everything is fixed and inevitable.

Do you know what today is?

– Somebody's *birthday*, he guessed.

She looked amused.

– A kind of birthday, she agreed: A New Year's Day.

The boy looked out of the balcony window down upon Rush Cutters Bay, where the yachts danced on the silver waters, and the high towers with reflecting orange glass in their windows rose behind them. What vegetation he could see was evergreen and confusing.

– You mean it's Spring? he asked.

But she had moved on.

– All my life Hans used my thoughts as he used his own pain. How can that be excused? He put out a travesty of my spirit into the world. And before the ink was dry, people were questioning me: Is it really true? You were so cross. So disobliging, so cruel?

She shrugged.

– We did not speak to Walter at Port Bou; but his correct little moustache, and tin glasses stick in my mind. Well. Who knows? Who gives up, who endures, who fails and forgets, what saves one man in the pit and sends another to his pistol? What kills? The answers to such mysteries are locked in our very cells; or else in each childhood either endured or enjoyed. They remain mysteries.

The boy looked disappointed, and said: I hoped there might be more. Some manuscript, some poems, letters perhaps?

– You have been spoiled by women, she sighed: Already I feel reluctant to disappoint you. And did I say there was

13

nothing? Hans once said to me: I should never have turned to you for insight. You've always been locked into a world of cause and effect. And it is possible. I offer no opinions. *But*, if you would like to look in a briefcase, I shall be glad to give it to you.

The boy was startled: I shall be enormously careful, he began.

– A gift, the woman repeated vigorously: It is my gift to you. Because you are beautiful, and who knows otherwise if I should ever have seen you, living here as I do in this antipodean wilderness?

Part Two

HANS WENDLER'S DIARY

'To the lover the loved one appears always as
solitary'
   Walter Benjamin

VIENNA: 1938

1 January

I do not usually keep a diary. But since my tongue catches on
every consonant, as I try to explain my life's perplexity from
a couch, my poor analyst has suggested I begin to do so in
writing. Something certainly must be done to break through
the new and terrifying block I have developed about lectur-
ing in public. Very well. The matter is too serious to refuse
even the most dubious remedy. The last two lectures of my
course in the Philosophy of Art had to be cancelled
altogether. It cannot be long before my stammering terror is
publicly exposed next term; I cannot prolong the excuse of
laryngitis forever.

Needless to say, the whole idea of turning to an analyst
springs from my wife Inge.

2 January

Inge has a warm heart. I know. I have always known. But
Inge's warm heart has never been much use to me. Sensitivity would have been preferable. I had every reason to
believe I was marrying a woman of sensitivity. Interested in
poetry. Language. And discussing such matters seriously. I
was mistaken.

Now I've heard it said that women lose interest in sex
when they get married. I can't say that for Inge. But certainly she lost interest in talking to me. In me altogether,
perhaps, I should say. Except as something to cling to at
night, and you might say the same for a hot water bottle. She
has stopped seeing me, really. I could be a pile of clothes or
papers for all the attention she gives me. I should explain:

17

she is very grand in such matters, and has always believed herself far above domestic work.

Not, of course, that she is lazy. Most of her energy goes, indeed, into work. *Her* work. That is, her own arcane, incomprehensible work in particle physics.

I am told she is highly regarded as a research scientist. Well, I have no means of discovering whether that is true or false. I regret to say that science has never excited me in the least. Anyway, she is a scientist, which is unusual enough in a woman; and possibly a distinguished figure in her field. I, on the other hand am a poet. Not a bad poet. There was a time when my work was highly regarded; but I am no longer vain enough to hope for much acclaim. How can anyone know? Poetry. Who believes in it? In any case, I keep myself going in a variety of part-time jobs, which bring little honour.

I cannot altogether blame Inge's impatience with the whole class of behaviour which is thought of as literature. In our corrupt modern age it may well be some dangerous fantasy land, where people can live out, like voyeurs, a life they would be afraid to lead. And if art is only talking about itself, what could be more pompous? Is it any wonder intelligent people have given up taking any writer seriously? Novelists are no closer to the sharp edge of life than poets.

My own books were doubtless too obscure to be thrown on any fire, but the silence that surrounds them is all the deeper.

3 January

Today I watched a young girl carrying her stack of books and settle at the table across from my own. My intense gaze must have woken her to my presence for she looked up. She looked straight at me. And then, she smiled a sad, tender smile. Filled with some loneliness I could only guess at. She was too young to be lonely, I thought, returning her smile.

18

And felt a thrill of disturbance that was not so much erotic as spiritually engaging. Tenderness. It was altogether missing in my life. And here was a young girl – I doubt if she is more than twenty-five, smiling tenderly at me. Only at me.

I hardly looked at her body, which was sensibly dressed for cold weather. It was her face that ensnared me. Gentle creature, I thought: how I wish I had someone to care for and protect. I could accept the blind or the lame or the sick, if their faces bespoke such sweetness.

Such a deep need. In the bend of her soft neck over her book, I sensed a solitary nature like my own, with the same necessity to love deeply and share thoughts with a fellow spirit.

4 January

Inge is the best friend I have in the world. Is it my fault that I no longer take much pleasure in making love to her? Take no pleasure is wrong, perhaps; the pleasure of the body is always functional; necessary even; but remote. There is no shiver of true desire in our approaches; no lyricism at the moment of submission; no transport in her evident delight. It is not simply domesticity as such. If I am to be honest, these thoughts of mine go back to our earliest encounters. We enjoyed a sibling passion. There has always been something almost incestuous in our love. We have become too close, with the years. Partly because she protects me? Perhaps. But truly she does not feel like a mother, not even a bad mother. We are too alike; we are evenly bad at the business of providing for one another's needs. And I have to fight to make her accept the most banal propositions; I spend myself in such arguments. She questions, turns, *destroys*, everything I say. Her logic is relentless; I cannot match her, even when I'm altogether certain that I am right.

Inge has never understood how different a human being I could have been, if she had not exacerbated even the *mildest*

19

attempt at aesthetic discussion. She once tried to tell me, poor bewildered creature, that she *too* needed encouragement in her worldly ambitions. But why should I not behave as other men do, why should I not be permitted to say I want this done, or that. Why am I alone in being denied the god-given licence to grumble?

Her family disapproved of me, naturally; but they were even more opposed to her scientific work.

They were a wealthy family, whose women were supposed to lace themselves tightly in silk and do good works with any energy they had remaining. When I first stepped over the threshold of their shining home, and took in the Biedermayer furniture, the collection of Hungarian folk art, the sheer wasteful grandeur of the apartment, I remember a sensation of overwhelming envy.

To say my family were poor in those days is to convey nothing. Everyone was starving. But my mother had no knack with food or money, and my father liked to gamble at cards, which indeed he often did at the Jewish social club round the corner. In the nature of things he must surely *sometimes* have won but we saw no pfennig of it. And when he lost, he shamelessly took whatever money there was in the house.

That he was out of work was no shame. Millions were out of work. Still, the bitterness in him fed on that. He was a man who had wanted to work hard, and had nothing to which he could turn his hand. Even in good times, he would have worked for any firm that employed him.

Inge's family must have shared the trouble of those days. But her mother was a shrewd woman. She kept a clean house, and made good soup out of vegetables. Who knows how some people manage better than others? Which is not to say that any member of Inge's family showed much interest in things of the mind and spirit.

I should never have had the nerve to propose marriage myself; it was Inge who took a wild fancy to me. At that time she loved music, film, theatre, even poetry; she would listen to me read aloud for hours. I could not understand quite why she seemed so determined to marry me.

Now I think she deliberately chose someone to whom she could feel of use. To whom she could offer a hand in rescue. And that, beautiful as she was, she shared some of the same terrible insecurities that I did. Being a poet and being a woman made us equally outsiders. We could not fit in any Biedermayer household.

And so we set up on our own; and remained intimately dependent on one another in spite of our very different spheres of activity. I was much more notably successful at first than she was; and she seemed to take great pleasure in it. Little enough she bothers now about what is happening to me. Or what is happening in the Faculty.

She sails on fearless, or so they tell me. And I deal with the schemers about me as best I can. She no longer has the time to care, perhaps. First it was the child, then her new job. I carry on working, nevertheless. My first lecture for the next semester is written as always; but I cannot touch the pages without trembling.

7 January

A late developer, of course. A sickly child, not delicate, which suggests a fine spirit, but simply subject to every germ that proliferated in my wretched home. And, no doubt of this at least, ill fated in my father. Red-faced, disappointed bigot, he used his malign tongue on every one of us. No one could have tried harder to sabotage my academic career. I learnt to smile from mother. A fake sweetness in my case; I cannot remember her well enough to be sure. In any case, I learnt the ease of seduction young. And if Inge was not precisely my physical type, she was handsome enough. It was the strength of her love that caught me; or I should hardly have chosen such an extraordinary woman. If indeed I chose at all. In my own defence, there was no sign then that she was to become eminent at anything.

9 January

My analyst is not pleased with my notes, though I thought them frank and open, not to say gross in part. I was a little ashamed of them. But he only wants to know about my mother and father.

There is nothing neurotic, I want to say, about hating a father like mine. I was beaten by broom handles, leather belts, and horny red hands more often than I can recall. His anger was always surprising to me. He was a butcher by trade; a thick-set, high-coloured man with a spade beard. Once it was for listening to the radio. I think it was French poetry; my father decided inexplicably that it was sent from the Devil.

My mother was from Poland, I believe, with surprisingly blonde hair and blue eyes. It is strange, now, when I visit her grave I can remember few examples of tenderness from her during my childhood. But then, my father was a brute to her above all. He had her in tears every night. Perhaps it was a substitute for sex?

I think very rarely of my family and never see them now.

10 January

I have always steered clear of politics. Any man who is not frightened of what may happen these days, is a fool. And further. All violence terrifies me.

Only yesterday, I was standing at the No. 5 bus stop with Stefan, a young pupil of mine, who has recently left his wife and children and is living like a wolf in any place he can find. He has no money whatsoever; and the thought of lending him some had just struck me, when he pointed across the road towards Heidi, his new blonde mistress. It must have been about five o'clock; that strange time, when shops flood the wet streets with reflections of their own electric splendours, and yet there is still an uneasy light from the sky itself.

As we watched, a young man we both knew joined her, and she greeted him with an innocent enough kiss, as far as I could judge. But Stefan went quite white with rage.

– The bitch! He screamed, and I could hear in his voice how long he had spent over his afternoon coffee with brandy: It's a deliberate humiliation.

From the rails at the other side of the street, a tram arrived, blue sparks above it; but he strode across nevertheless. For a moment the tram hid the pavement altogether. Then I heard the bell, and the grinding rails as the tram moved away. And I saw to my bewilderment that Heidi was lying on the ground in front of Stefan who would not allow her to regain her feet. As I stared, a passing stranger tried to restrain Stefan; and received a blow in the face for his trouble. I could see his broken spectacles fall to the ground and blood pouring from his eyes.

– What are you doing? I yelled angrily. I could do no more, for the traffic was too dense to cross the road. And so I had to watch another vicious kick to the girl's head, and God knows what other damage would not have been done if a policeman had not sauntered on to the scene.

By the time I reached the brawl, the policeman was writing notes in a book, while the girl sobbed miserably on the wet ground. Whatever he had been asking her, she agreed, and her answers seemed to satisfy him. My pupil turned his indignation on the policeman.

– What does any of this matter? She is a whore. Putting her filthy tongue into a stranger's mouth. Right in front of me.

– Calm yourself down, the policeman suggested, without any of the indignation I might have expected. It was as if the hatred men feel for women, even those they have wronged, was too commonplace to pursue. Catching my eye, he hesitated and, almost as if apologizing, added: Everyone quarrels when they are drunk.

When I described the incident to Inge, her glacial contempt quite unjustly accused me of doing less than I should.

12 January

Perhaps if Inge knew some of the difficulties I have with Kurt we would be closer. I mean, however much they were predictable, ill judged, all my own fault. What has happened to me through Kurt is none the less a betrayal.

Among the rest of the preposterous ill-paid nonsense I spend my life upon, one, small enjoyable hour is the class I give in Ethics as part of the University Department of Fine Arts. The Director must once have read my early poems, I believe. For three years now, I have been able to enjoy a small, but regular stipend, for a decent, honourable chore.

The class itself was undeniably a little stodgy. (Students with more talent would have been put into the Professor's class.) So when a young son of an old friend of mine presented himself to me, I was entirely flattered. He had few qualifications, but his mother had been talented; a clever actress. And I was happy to have him in my class.

He was very much like his mother as I remembered her; narrow-featured, with jet black eyes that glittered with a malice which was, for some reason, attractive rather than alarming. At least, I found it so at first; before I understood what was happening.

My stammer (at that time little more than a slight hovering over certain difficult words) was never remarked upon by the students. For my part, I was delighted to welcome an eloquent student. I did not see how he threw my own sober, honest sentences into shadow beside his brilliance. In plain terms, he decided to seduce my class from me; and it was through him I first heard ripples of laughter that were no longer tolerant but antagonistic.

14 January

I have never had much faith in miracles; though Inge claims it is the poet's province. But today I must confess I opened my mail and revised that opinion. Some group has read an early poetic play of mine and wants my permission to stage it in Paris. It is true no money is mentioned; and for all I know the group is drawing audiences of less than a dozen. I looked the play out again, however. Yes. It has a certain style, an edge, some tang of the sketches so successful at the *Simplicissimus*. And, of course, there are many German émigrés in Paris now.

15 January

I have looked at the letter again, and I am by no means sure that anything definite has been proposed. Inge claims that the French use subjunctives only as a form of politeness. But I have been betrayed by her optimism before. Why is she so sure of everything when she is so often wrong? Even if I were cautious for no other reason, her unquestioning delight would be sufficient reason for alarm. After all, who is to say it is not a trick? I searched all morning for the envelope in which the magical letter arrived, to make sure at least it had been posted in France. In some insane fit of tidiness, it has been thrown away. Inge says she looked very closely at the postmark before giving it to me. She cannot understand why I don't believe her. I was forced to cancel the first seminar of the term.

16 January

I have formed the clear intention of not replying to the letter.
If it's a serious offer, they will know how things stand in
Vienna now. An Austrian passport deserves to be zealously
guarded.

17 January

Inge left yesterday. She will be away ten days at a Scientific
Congress in Berlin, which I must say seems selfish, consider-
ing my condition.

I looked at her closely, my Inge, with her amber eyes
and aquiline face, and speculated. Was she perhaps contem-
plating a little sexual adventure? I could hardly blame her.
Women age so much more unfairly than men. At forty, she
was still in the prime of her life; and fidelity is not much
valued in our circle. There is something too straitlaced in
her, however, some cowardice which would probably prevent her responding boldly. I know she is lonely in her own
way. But then. It was her idea to send the child away to
America, last July; the very day after Germany promised not
to interfere in Austrian afairs. I suppose she must miss him
terribly. I cannot say I feel so strongly. To tell the truth I
shall be quite pleased to have a few days alone.

I took her to the station; and on my return, to my astonishment, there was another letter from Paris. Well, the offer
seems to be serious. For some reason, which I cannot
altogether fathom, I was pleased that the offer had come to
me in Inge's absence. Why do I feel so much more excitement? It is my offer. Not our offer.

I shall send her a telegram with the news nevertheless. She
will be pleased and proud. I'm a child! She could perhaps
investigate a little. They claim to number some of Brecht's
own group among them.

8 February

I went in to work at the Library as usual.

12 February

So our Chancellor Schusschnigg has paid a friendly call on Hitler. And yet everything remains normal. No one seems particularly alarmed, even the few outright Jews who remain in the University. An exception is Gerhardt Brandt, who has quietly applied for his US visa. As a physicist, of course, he will have no difficulty. But for a poet; it is a kind of suicide.

Am I making a fuss? Gerhardt is remarkably plausible, I am haunted by his simian face. He assured me that everyone in the Jewish community at least could read the cards now; the little tea party had included enough jackbooted generals to spell out Hitler's true meaning. And how could we trust any government that contained von Seyss-Inquart?

I said I hardly knew what he meant. Though of course I knew the name as the leader of the Nationalist Opposition.

– You will see, he nodded.

– Schushnigg is an academic, I began.

– Exactly. Which is not what is needed to deal with Hitler.

He then told me some gossip of how Hitler had treated his so-called friend and ally. I did not see how he could know so much, and said so.

Everyone is preoccupied with his own private agony. It is common knowledge that Gerhardt will soon be removed from his post as a radical.

13 February

I can no longer disguise the fact that Kurt is trying to destroy me. Why? Why? I cast my mind back to my dealings with his mother. It is true we were one-time lovers; but it was not a passion that went deeply on either side. For a moment, I wondered whether he suspected I was his true father? Could his mother have suggested as much? But the dates would be wrong.

Yesterday, I determined to make a real attempt to grasp the nature of his hostility. I invited him to the Reiss Bar in one of the streets of Karntnerstrasse. The bar is all shiny mahogany, red leather and chrome. He grimaced when I suggested the rendezvous: A place of whores, he said.

— Not in the middle of the day. We can sip a liqueur. Talk, I pleaded.

— Very well, he agreed indifferently.

There was only one waiter; and no girls, I was glad to see. Upon our arrival the waiter put on the radio which played light music of depressing sweetness.

Well, I had planned everything I was going to say. That there was no truth that I could see in the letter Kurt had recently written to the Director. In what sense could my lectures be said to undermine the morale of the class? It was true I had some difficulty in speaking clearly; but surely nothing I said could be construed as polluting young Austria? Looking at him across the table, I felt my confidence dwindle. I drained my first schnapps to give me courage; while he still looked down at his, thoughtfully.

— Have I harmed you in some way I don't know? I began abruptly and not at all as I intended.

Kurt only smiled at me.

— Personalities don't come into it. You are polluting our homeland, he said.

My neck froze at the newspaper phrase.

— Pollute? How so?

He wagged his finger at me, like a Swiss burgher.

— We shall have no more mongrels soon.

— Inge, I began.

— I am not talking about your wife.

As soon as he said that I was afraid to probe further. The knowing malevolence in his eyes seemed too formidable.

I wanted to ask his own politics; and did not dare. I voted for Schusschnigg; whom did he favour?

– What are you asking me to do?

– You should leave, he said, still smiling.

– You want my post. Is that it? I shouted. I shouted mainly because it was only the sudden burst of anger that had freed my tongue at all.

– I have been ill, I said sombrely.

– Illness is something we shall have no time for, he said.

And I still had no idea whether he was speaking for a group on the left or the extreme right. I was too frightened to ask.

He rose, leaving his brandy untouched. When I was sure he had left the bar altogether, I furtively exchanged glasses. But even the brandy could not prevent me shaking.

14 February

Today my analyst wrote to cancel our appointment. He says he is ill; but I have a different theory. In our last session, he was decidedly inattentive. (And I had a most interesting dream; very rare for me. My dear dead mother had turned into a black owl, and hooted a warning from a tree.) It is true the man asked to see my diary but I had the distinct impression that he leafed through without much consideration.

I am not a fool, and do not propose to confide all my thoughts to my analyst. Damn him, I found myself thinking with a peculiar sense of liberation. At least, I shall be spared his strictures this week.

It would not bother me in the least if I stopped seeing him altogether. My professor confided to me only the other day that no one believes in psychoanalysis any more and whispered they might soon be outlawed as quacks.

I remember when Herr von Neurath, the German Foreign Minister, came to visit Vienna last year. I stood in the crowds to watch. He was such a reassuringly silver-haired gentleman, a German aristocrat as one likes to think of them; I was only sorry that Inge was not at my side to witness his descent. I was a little surprised when he greeted our waiting Austrian diplomats with a brisk 'Heil Hitler' and the Nazi salute; but I suppose it is by now a mere figure of speech. I confess his rising arm disturbed me as much as the enthusiastic crowds that responded. But Austria is not Germany, whatever these thugs may like to believe.

15 February

Today. How shall I describe today? I rose with my extraordinary sense of freedom still with me, and walked out into the wintry Vienna streets towards the Library. The sky was blue, and the whole world had a crisp, glittering beauty. The snow sat in the crotches of the cherry trees like blossom. I felt clean and young and filled with poetry.

And then, who should join me at my sunlit table but the very girl I have been staring at so intensely for the last few weeks. And it was she who spoke first.

It was a young, sweet voice, as tender as her face; and the pleasure was so intense that for a moment I did not catch the words, delivered as they were in French.

Thinking herself misunderstood, she repeated them in German: You have been watching me. I suppose you remember where we met?

I had no such memory; but I could feel my lips open sweetly in a smile. Perhaps the whole world was about to begin again?

Naturally I did not refuse the simple occasion for intimacy she offered.

– You will let me buy your tea? And perhaps an apple pie?
– I never eat much, she said.

It was what I expected her to say. Food was a gross, Biedermayer passion. My only worry was the excitement, and the effect it might have on my uncertain voice control.

Speak to me again in French, I wanted to say; because my heart was squeezed with the kind of poignant joy I remembered most sharply from French films. German was a hard language, and it did not suit her gentle tongue.

– Will you let me know your name?

– Hilde, she said promptly.

– At my age I forget names.

She laughed: But you can't be more than forty.

At this I could feel my back straightening, and I probably put up my hand to straighten my hair and touch my tie. It was a pity Inge had forgotten to collect the dry cleaning before she left. At least she could have left me the ticket. How unfair that I should be in an old jacket and trousers.

Inge is not a willing creature. I remembered her face with a certain sadness. Partly to assuage a sense of what I wanted. I thought particularly of that myopic bewildered stare she turns on me when she is crossed. Her friends have described her eyes to me as mournful, or even warmly loving. Well, every man must meet the eyes he sees, and they are not often turned in warmth and love upon me.

My fault, you will say. Well, I do not deny the brutalities in my own behaviour. I don't deny I have been, shall we say, *unfeeling*, myself. A man has to be taught to feel, if he comes from a home like mine.

Partly to cure my nervousness, I selected a good piece of Schwarzwald cake; and then cursed myself for such gross overeating. To my surprise, Hilde said as much immediately, as if we were in telepathic communications.

– A handsome man like you should not allow yourself to become overweight.

I found myself smiling at her mischievously.

– Sometimes it is necessary to celebrate. She looked sad at that, and it occurred to me that she was someone of whom I knew nothing at all; for all I knew her parents might have been whisked off in the middle of the night. Perhaps there had been a lover's quarrel. I looked at her hands. There was

31

a simple gold band on the forefinger of her right hand. She was married, I guessed. It was no answer to feeling unhappy.

The urge to comfort the girl was so powerful that I was furious to find a friend of mine taking a seat at the table with us. He was, moreover, a brooding fellow from the South, and a friend of Inge's too.

– How is the new book of poems going, Hans?

– Slowly. As ever, I replied, my spirits drooping a little. I had almost forgotten the book I am supposed to be preparing.

– Did you read of the happenings last night? he asked.

I was momentarily surprised. My friend is not much of a newspaper reader normally.

It seems there was a public rally outside the Parliament buildings to protest against the number of foreigners trying to escape over our frontier.

– Criminals, in flight from Germany, he said. His eyebrows rose as he called them *criminals*; but I did not respond to the implied irony, even though his eyes sought mine with a desperation, that reminded me of *Ostjuden* huddling in their slums. On any other day, I would have tried to reassure him; but it was impossible in front of Hilde. Luckily, he got up soon and left, without much of a friendly word in farewell.

And then I turned and looked into Hilde's eyes; which were as pale as muscat wine; and to my own astonishment I began to confess everything to her that was making me unhappy. My father seemed a good place to begin. And it turned out, miraculously, to be an affliction she shared with me. She, too, had been beaten by broom handles and leather belts; she, too, had lost her mother young.

There and then, sitting in that cold, ill-lit room, I confessed to my speech impediment. I even admitted to my terror of giving the first lecture of the term.

– You could practise it with me, she murmured.

– In your flat? She smiled and nodded. We did not speak of Inge; but she must have known I was married.

16 February

Chaque époque rêve la suivante.

> Michelet

So I began to read my paper aloud to Hilde, who sat adoringly at my feet. My voice was fluent and steady.

– The ruins of modernity, I said. And she sighed and looked up as if what I spoke had been transfigured into a sensuous lyric. I paused, and almost without thinking put a hand on her soft, baby-clean hair. Inge's hair was crinkly under my hand, like a monkey's, I often thought unkindly; just as her face was tinged with yellow and there was always something indoor and sour about her whole person that the heavy perfumes she preferred seemed only to enhance.

And here was a snub-nosed girl of twenty-five with her yellow hair against my thigh, looking up at me and understanding all the ideas I had tried out so often on Inge, to find them falling dead at my feet.

The girl could not have heard what I read to her with more delight if it had been a love poem. I was not stupid. I could feel my penis rising as I read (so near her hair, so close to those adoring, uncoloured pink lips). Her idolatry was intoxicating; and if I continued to read the paper rather than bending there and then to make love to her, it was because there was something so deeply sensual in our sitting together it was as sweet as copulation.

I knew we would exchange souls. I had a boundless trust in the consequence of such love. And I loved everything about her room, which was different from my own. I never liked the smell of any house we lived in. With such certainty of joy only a moment's thought stayed me. I had an appointment with the Director early the following morning and would need clean clothes. (Later it struck me as an act of extraordinary prescience that Hilde had clean underclothes and a shirt of my correct size laid out ready for me. Marvellous creature.)

– Grandiose and grotesque, I concluded. And for a moment, looking down, I wondered if, after all, it was the woman in her I had stirred.

– Wonderful, she breathed: So lucid, so brilliant.

It came to me with great precision that I had never been understood so clearly by Inge in the whole of our marriage.

18 February

Inge arrived home. To my horror, she looks ill and shaken. At first, she would say nothing except that Berlin had frightened her. Uneasily, I wondered if rumours of my behaviour had reached her. I hoped not; I don't know why, but it seemed important.

She sat smoking a cigarette; and I offered her a brandy. Only then did she begin to speak, in a shrill, frightening voice. I thought she must have taken leave of her senses. Berlin was relatively calm, she insisted; there were still Jewish shops open on the main shopping streets, and although there were many yellow stars, things had not been as bad as she feared.

But her cousins had been picked up.

– For what?

– As Jews, she said.

I laughed. Her family had been baptised Catholics for nearly a century. It was a comic blunder. She flinched at my laughter.

– Supposing I took a job in Paris? Would you come with me?

– You can't be serious.

– Listen, she said: Both my mother's parents are buried in Jewish holy ground. That is enough for the Nazis.

– Well, enough for what?

– To be taken away, to be put in a camp, perhaps abused. There are worse rumours. And what of your own roots, Hans?

I was very angry: I hope you won't throw my parents' origins in my face.

– Hans, I have always known you didn't wish me to speak of it. I have always avoided the subject. But surely now you can see we must be honest, at least with one another? Your mother came from Poland. I have always known your origins, Hans. Why do you imagine I am the only one?

– I am altogether German, I shouted: What should I do in Paris?

– As much as you do here.

– Why should we run away like cowards?

I should be leaving Hilde behind, I realized suddenly, and perhaps that gave some genuine conviction to my voice.

– Well, Hans. We should not be the first to leave. Thomas Mann left long ago; and Hannah Arendt; and Brecht.

– I am not a left-winger.

– As a writer, exile is difficult, she said. Then sighed.

For a moment, I thought she might be suspicious, after all. Then I saw her eyes were filled with tears.

– You are not a fool. You must see the danger. I had not expected you to be so brave. Very well. If you wish it so, we will stay.

She bent over to kiss me, and I drew in an acrid breath of smoke and cognac.

– Good night.

19 February

Inge is once again a whirl of activity, suspecting nothing. There are so many kinds of betrayal.

Spice. Inge has always found spice in others, and not in me. It does not matter that it isn't erotic. She gives them her energy, and nothing is left for me. Long ago, as I stopped writing poems, as I began to wither and die, she watched indifferently. Now I have begun to write again, she observes no change. I feel as full of poems, as if my new love drew them from me as easily as she draws my passion. I am not ashamed. Sex is not the only kind of infidelity. And when I question Inge about her lunches with friends, she finds only petty curiosity in my interest. Wrong. And bitter. Jealousy is an emotion a man may forgive; it has its place, its dignity, it leaves a man whole and hard. But an interest in gossip?

She understood nothing; her own infidelity went too deep. She couldn't help it, couldn't help me. As my life dwindled, as I became a hack journalist, whose poetry no one remembered. How easily she went on saying, 'But I love you. Only you.'

Now I hold Hilde in my arms, and I do not need that love. I am returned to life. And the source of creation.

20 February

Inge and I listened to Hitler for the first time broadcasting on Austrian radio. Thundering Seig Heils! greeted his arrival as we had expected. But then he devoted most of his speech to the economic miracles achieved under his stewardship. He barely referred to the Jewish question; there were no denunciations of Bolsheviks either.

– Well, I said, as if confirmed in my opinions. Neither of us could deny the feeling of relief. When I met Brandt later in the day, I made a great deal of the news that Bruno Walter's contract with the Vienna Opera had been renewed for a year.

22 February

For the first time I stayed out until nearly morning, without any explanation to Inge. We spent a long while talking. I remember saying to Hilde: How did I waste the first forty years of my life without you?

— Now we shall be happy, the girl encouraged me.

— You will not love me long.

— As long as we live, she said quietly: How she has hurt you, that arrogant bitch of a wife. Why?

— No, I said: Not arrogant.

— She doesn't see you, she has left you alone following her own career.

I shifted uncomfortably, because she had picked up my criticism just a shade too easily, and I was anxious, thinking of Inge alone at home.

— I have also made her miserable, I said at length: She is a kind of human being you don't understand, my love. She is genuinely without calculation.

— How appalling, she said: And without the slightest care for you.

— We neglected one another equally, I tried to explain.

— Look at her clothes. The way she stands. Her joy in her celebrity.

— She doesn't think like that.

— You'll be telling me next she is good, murmured my beloved Hilde.

— Yes, I said, relieved: That's it. She is.

To my horror, I found Inge was still awake as I let myself in. Dressed and awake and yet bleary, as if she had spent the night pacing.

— My God, what has happened? I asked stupidly. She flung her arms round me, and sobbed as if her heart would break.

— I thought you were dead.

— Look, you don't usually wait up for me. How could I guess? I remonstrated practically.

— Hans, I have given in my resignation to the lab, she said: I have been here all day waiting to tell you. And then, as I

37

waited through the whole evening, I became convinced. They would take out my foolishness on you.

– Resign? I held on to the only bewildering word I could make out of the blur of her speech.

– They have appointed a monster in place of Brandt. I have resigned in protest.

– And Brandt?

She seemed to collect herself, then her eyes looked me over closely.

– Where *have* you been? she asked me directly.

– Talking.

– Until six in the morning? She asked me.

– Yes.

She raised her eyes incredulously.

Suddenly I was desperately tired.

– Come, she said softly, and we went to bed and wound our arms about each other.

My heart banged uncomfortably. In my mind, I turned over what I should tell Hilde.

23 February

A restless weekend. As far as I can tell, Inge has decided to let the matter of my night away from home pass without further comment. A great relief, but I wish Hilde understood how important *caution* is to me now. One or two of my men friends have already hinted that they know more of my affairs than I guess. Worse, Kurt dropped in to deliver an essay which he particularly wanted me to read. (Damned boy. Why should his respect still flatter me?) And as he left, he too murmured something about Hilde's wild past. Something dangerous and political and quite invented I dare say.

24 February

I looked at myself for a long while in the mirror, and tried to imagine how Hilde could prefer me to admirers close to her own age. If my old therapist had not disappeared, I would have put the matter to him quite frankly. One piece of good fortune: The University does not seem to question my absence for the moment.

25 February

Inge is agitated today both about friends in France, and others returning to the Soviet Union. It is rumoured Brecht is among them. Her own hope in Russia died with the Moscow trials; but some people are endlessly gullible. But she still puts some faith in French Socialism. She argues it is now a question of Trade Unions in France, and that social reform is the order of the day. Don't I approve of better hours, paid holidays and so forth? The danger in her eyes comes always from the Right: Action Française. The Catholic literary intellectuals.

— Why literary? I would have liked to ask.

— Listen, she said. And told me more about the well-springs of hatred; the Mouvement Anti-Juif Continental, the weekly *Gringoire*, not to mention *Candide*, and what more suitable name? That villain Voltaire. As if anyone would condemn Voltaire for one idiosyncratic prejudice.

— I don't know what is best, she said: At least the French hate the Germans. All this year the mood has been growing darker in Paris.

— Mark my words, she said: By next month we shall have Germans in Austria. Hans, please. Let us leave while we still can.

I was tempted, not so much by her arguments; but by the thought that, after all, I should not arrive altogether a nobody. Not only was my play to be performed, but the group were happy to pay me a sizeable fee. On the other hand, I did not want to leave Hilde.

— Why don't you go ahead now? I suggested.

I swear I was not thinking of getting her out of the way, but allaying her anxieties. But even as I promised to follow, as soon as I could arrange something, her mouth closed into a tight line.

– I don't agree it is a good idea to separate.

– This would not be a separation in the ordinary sense, I said smiling.

– A separation is a separation. I know you, Hans, she said.

And for a moment I realized that it was true, in a sense, but what Inge knows is only the *worst* in me, the pettiest and the least interesting.

– Do I grudge you your women friends? I asked.

– How is that to the point? she glared at me. It was an old story.

– To be sure, in this world there is no eternal love. Even ordinary faithfulness is out of the way. Perhaps women sustain one another against that knowledge, that vulnerability. But there is nothing erotic in my friendship with women, said Inge sullenly. I knew it was true. Her narrow figure, slim hips, and proud head attracted other women; but she had never wanted their love.

It was a fantasy of mine that there was something masculine about her. But if there was any truth in it, it was not a matter of hormones. She knew more than other women; she seemed too strong. And she earnt a man's wage.

When I was angry, I sometimes searched her top lip, which even in her forties was unmarked by hair, and accused her of plucking out the evidence.

Today, I tried to soothe her. She is losing weight, I observed.

She coughed several times and found difficulty catching her breath.

– It will be my death, she said. Without explanation.

26 February

Disturbed today. On my walk to the library I passed a figure that seemed half-familiar to me; as if, in another context, I might even know him very well. The man had grey hair, and an overcoat of brown herringbone tweed, belted at the waist with a knot of string. Under his arm he was carrying several rolled newspapers. The shabbiness of his clothes suggested madness more than poverty. And his little eyes darted about as fiercely as the arm that held the newspapers was pressed to his side.

He seemed to be walking with a determination not to fall apart; and this impression was increased when, to my surprise, he reached the street where a few cars were parked close by the old police station. In spite of the filth and rust that must have spattered his coat, he forced his old body tight up to the wall. I could see he was panting a little, and was a little afraid he might actually stick half-way and have to be dragged out. But he pulled his chest in, and his belly, and his face reddened with the effort and then he was through. And then I recognized him. He was my old analyst. Something terrible had certainly happened to him. I did not risk finding out what it was.

27 February

How shall I live this down? How shall I bear it? Today I attempted to give my second lecture. It goes without saying that I had brought not only comprehensive notes, but also the most varied and widely drawn quotations to read, just in case I found myself undergoing the terrible vocal paralysis of the preceding term. My pulse rate was high, but all began well enough, though I saw Kurt in the audience, grinning, as if waiting for my collapse.

There was a slight breathiness in my voice such as might accompany ordinary nervousness. But I felt confident enough to make the traditional request for hands to be held up by those who found me inaudible.

I then began to read a quotation from Spinoza, my head poised over the page so that every period should be correctly pointed, and every word enunciated as it should be. I only lifted my head at the end of Spinoza's paragraph.

And what did I see then but a forest of hands. They extended, not only from the back three rows where the acoustics are admittedly tricky, but up to the very first bench. For one moment, I had the exact sense of being caught up in a dream. On stage in an opera perhaps (I cannot sing a note), or in a foreign play; or perhaps in some familiar piece, where the action leads up to my speech but I have forgotten.

I laughed, a little feebly.

And then I saw Kurt's face. And some of his friends were standing in the gangways. They stood there, with arms folded, and waited, until every arm in the room rose into what was more or less the Nazi salute.

I wanted to say many things. Simple things. For example, that it is forbidden to stand in gangways. The University expressly forbids it. That Spinoza (if such was their objection) had been cast out by his own community. But no word came out of my lips.

It must have been then I noticed Hilde, who was sitting on the bench below Kurt.

It looked to me as if, when he leaned forward, his hand touched her head. Of course, it is impossible to be sure, because it was at that precise moment I pitched forward in a dead weight down the steps of the podium, and crashed into the blackness.

I am writing this from my hospital bed. Inge brought in my diary without comment. I cannot tell if she has read it.

— Luckily, it is your left arm that is broken, she said.

Can she really be so unfeeling?
They have told me I shall be home in a week.

28 February

Two things have bewildered me today. Hilde has left for France with no more than a note saying that she loves me as passionately as ever; and when can I join her? This has frightened me more than anything yet.

Inge saw my pale face, and imagined it had something to do with our neighbours; the Bratsky family, who completed their arrangements for leaving yesterday. I was sorry for them, they looked so pale and wretched. Of course. Bratsky lost his University post. Something political, it is said. They say Bratsky has been secretly transferring funds to a Swiss bank account for years. Although they have been our neighbours these last ten years I feel little in common with them. Why do these people cling so to their religion? As if it hadn't been proved time and time again that God takes no care of anyone.

Inge seems to be disproportionately distressed. In fact, I am just a little worried about her. She has lost more weight, and has no appetite. I blame her quixotic gesture. It makes no sense; and endangers both of us. Inge said drily: It is as well we were once a family with two incomes.

She has not mentioned leaving Vienna again, I'm glad to say. The general consensus, even among outright Jews of my acquaintance, is that Hitler cannot last much longer. Even if those who might have kept him in check have failed; now he is going to extremes, the people never will follow him.

1 March

A blowy day, with few signs of Spring. I had arranged to take Hilde to Switzerland this weekend. Unlike Inge, who has no real interest in anything outside major cities, Hilde

43

loves Nature as I do. We had planned to meet again on neutral territory for a short walking excursion, which she has called off. She was rather mysterious about her reasons. I pressed her, for some reason; the face of Kurt was present very vividly to my mind as I stared into the black telephone. But she seemed genuinely surprised. The reason has to do with only herself and me. I don't know why my heart sank at the phrasing. I did not know how to explain how much I would prefer if she kept our relationship secret; but it seemed mealy-mouthed to do so.

When I asked Inge if she would (since the hotel is booked) like to come away for a weekend to Interlaken with me, she burst out crying. I was appalled. Apparently, she took the offer as a serious renewal of love. Perhaps, in part, she was right. And indeed as we walked through the Spring grass, the turf bouncy under our heels, and I watched Inge striding ahead with an impatient spirit, I *did* acknowledge how deep an affection I felt for her. It occurred to me then, that, whatever happened, I could not manage without her. Hilde was one thing; and this was another. I could not manage without either or them. I would have liked to say as much, when we were in bed, in our mountain chalet. Inge lay open-eyed, staring at a gathering storm about the ice peaks above us.

– Blue lightning, she murmured.

– You are my true family, all the family I have ever had, I exclaimed.

And then she was silent for a long time in the dark, and I did not know what she was thinking.

We prolonged our stay for a week. I realized that, as much as anything else, I did not want to return to Hilde's news.

3 March

We came home to a pile of mail; one in Hilde's handwriting. I put it first to one side; then in my pocket, in the hope it would escape Inge's attention.

Then I went anxiously in to the lavatory to read Hilde's letter. To my enormous relief, there was no sign of the crisis she had suggested over the telephone. Was it possible I could plan to take the evening train to Paris on Tuesday?

I came down again, feeling freer; and caught a glimpse of Inge's face, as she proceeded stolidly to open her own letters, one after the other. There is something archaic about that expression, I thought; an archaic strength, as if she had an Egyptian in her family tree.

Her eyes looked up as they felt mine upon her; and I dropped my own before the inquiry in their gaze.

45

Part Three
INGE WENDLER'S DIARY

'Natural guilt . . . befalls man not on account of
action and decision but through idleness and
hesitation'
   Walter Benjamin

PARIS: 1938

3 September

Hans has been so elated by the success of his play, that he walks like another man. He strides about our rooms, whistling, as if he owned the whole world; as if our friends still in Austria were not being horribly abused and tormented. I don't grudge him the happiness, but I resent the frivolity. When I say so, he laughs and says: Write more letters, Inge. Perhaps you will find a job, after all.

I write letters every day. It has not been easy. We are thought of as aliens, here in Paris; there were too many physicists from Germany already. To be German, and a woman, and now to be counted as Jewish: these are handicaps.

And whatever rewards Hans' play may have brought him, the money was no fortune; and I am told the piece will be taken off any day now. Our savings, which I was lucky to get out of the country, cannot last forever. When I say as much, Hans nods, and seems to know; but his thoughts are elsewhere. He is living in a dream.

We arrived in Paris only days before the *Anschluss*. Chance, Hans calls it. It is possible. He has no idea what it would mean to apply that principle to the universe I once investigated daily. When I try to explain, he falls into bored preoccupation. He has never understood the relevance of magnetic fields to the God in his poems, never seen any relevance to the human heart in the laws by which the atoms move. And yet he asks himself whether we are creatures with whom God is amusing himself, as if at a dice.

I have spoken to enough refugees from Germany now to

understand what horrors we escaped. People who left Germany six years ago still speak of their experience with fear.

And then, from the personal point of view, I am happy whenever I think we have left behind whatever entanglement my poor Hans had found himself so caught in before we came away.

6 September

Hans' friend, Hilde, has found us a cheap room in the Marais with some Jewish friends of hers. Convenient as it is for the moment, I gather she herself is living in some splendour near Les Invalides. Not for the first time, I wonder why she has chosen to run away from the Nazis. I have satisfied myself she is not even partly Jewish.

Someone, certainly, is supporting her. I observe it is the latter suggestion which produces spasms of indignation in him.

These days I do not even dare to cry.

10 September

I am grateful that I brought the letters from our son Frederick with us. It was an impulse rather than foresight. They were so painful to me, those first bewildered letters from his twelve-year-old pen: resentful, fearful, unexpectedly bossed by my cousins in their Los Angeles suburban home. How strange he found American schooling. How he was unused to being at the bottom of the class. To hear music ridiculed by quite intelligent children; to be so lonely, so terribly in need of love.

It used to squeeze my heart every time I looked at them. Only this year did he begin to write coolly, and often in English.

Hans used to blame me for sending him away; but even if I never live to see him again (and these last few days I have been choking with some bronchitic infection, I cannot imagine how I will get through the winter) even then I rejoice to think he has been released from this European dungeon. Because, for all the pleasure Hans takes in it, and for all the splendours of its gay heart, Paris as we live in it is a dungeon.

I have sent Frederick our new address, but so far there has been no word.

10 September

I like the district: cobbles, narrow streets, continuous bustle, unfamiliar smells. A butcher's shop round the corner sells goods, cheap offal, even spleen; I wish I had room enough in the gas stove to cook it as it should be prepared.

The attic room is small, with room for only one desk. Yesterday rain brought down the plaster over the bed. I wash clothes in the sink downstairs; it's not such a hardship. The other lodgers are friendly; many of them refugees as bewildered by their situation as we are.

12 September

Last night, we went to see a group of German students in *Faust*. A marvellous play. Hans has often explained all its ambiguities to me. Tonight he seemed fascinated. Particularly by the girl who plays Margarita. Certainly she is a particularly beautiful actress. They are all students, none of them more than twenty-two or twenty-three. Afterwards, we went to the theatre backstage, which we can do as members of the University. It was Hans' idea; I wanted to please him, but I was tired. I said so.

– When are you *not* tired? When were you *ever* young? he demanded: I want to have a drink at the bar and see if that

51

girl is as sensitive to speak with as she seems on the stage.
You can go home if you like.

As I sit shuddering, at the wall, I watch the ease with
which he picks her up. No stammering in these situations I
thought bitterly. No fear, even as he looks at her first shyly,
then slyly; soon he buys them both a drink. For twenty
minutes or so, he turns all the benevolence of his face upon
her. That night, as we were dropping off to sleep, he said: 'I
have never loved you enough, and that is what I am being
punished for.'

– Punished? I asked, puzzled. But he is asleep and doesn't
answer.

16 *September*

I do not know what to do about Hans' *affaire*, which
continues, he maintains, only as friendship. The pain of it
puzzles my head.

– Why didn't you tell me? I asked.

– I didn't want it to spoil our love, he said. I could only
gaze at him with incredulity.

– It's over, he said: I promise you.

– Really? I wanted to believe him. There was enough in
the newspaper to frighten us into closeness again.

– Look at what has been happening in Vienna! They have
old women mopping up streets. And such delight in looting
and rape. Always rape.

He sighed. But I could tell the shadow that crossed his
face was from another threat.

– Have you arranged to see her again? I asked him,
evenly.

– See who?

I knew he understood, and shrugged. So that he was
forced to reply.

– Yes. Listen. Trust me. Will you trust me?

I didn't see what sense it made but I nodded.

– Surely you can trust me for one night?

My heart ran cold again.

– To be out all night?

I hated to be alone in the flat, and of all times now.

– Not alone of course, he reassured me: Look, I'll arrange for my brother to call round, he has sent his wife to England. Such a graceful woman you know. A mistake . . .

I murmured something: *Why* all night?

– Trust me. Believe me.

Almost I did believe him.

– She can do us terrible damage.

– Politically?

– Perhaps.

– How? Is she *mad*? Or what?

– A little mad, he said: Please. Think of this as some little lie you might tell me about the butcher's bill to keep me happy. When you do that it is to protect me, isn't it?

– You are going to *her*, tonight, to protect *me*? *How*?

– Trust me.

Suddenly I didn't believe him at all. I said: What worse can she do? You don't deny she is your mistress.

– Worse. Much worse. Darling.

Reluctantly I let him go, and with him the whole peace of my mind.

His brother came late and hungry, and expecting more than the cold supper I had provided. I could hardly bear to talk to him. In dim lights, the resemblance to Hans was close enough to disturb me; but I did not see what else there was in the world to talk about.

He on the contrary was filled with gossip. Did I know that? And that? And had Hans and I yet taken the necessary steps for?

We have done none of these things; poor improvident creatures and I was glad to see him go.

Hell. I am in Hell. I suppose he is with her now. And I don't know and can't know, what is really going on, or what is the nature of this terrifying power which he so fears, and which he will not even put into words. To protect me? How many more grey nights, sleepless and waiting must I bear with the question that he will never answer.

Dear Lord, what is to become of us? Does he know how frightened I am? He says that *I* am real, and I haven't lost him, and yet. What does he tell *her*? What has he promised *her*? She has summoned him to her and he obeys. What are they doing? Does he not, frankly, find it more entertaining with her? Will she bind him to her with sex, and youth, and lively conversation?

— I'm slowly disentangling, he says.

Why slowly?

When at last he returned, it was morning again and I had begun to cry with a wild abandon I knew must be close to madness.

— Must you do that? he asked.

There are women who can look enticing when they weep, but my own animal abandon frightened me as well as repelling him. What if I lost my senses altogether? How could such a situation be coped with?

— There, there, he said awkwardly. And I heard the falsity in his voice: We'll work out something, you'll see. Some compromise.

— Never, I shrieked. Never. I won't be condemned to that.

And then I began to moan: What's to become of me? What's to become of me?

Hans appears to me now to have been the centre of my life all the time. Not my work, as I had imagined. How could he not know the difference in me?

When I tried to explain as much, he looked sardonically upon me, and inquired whether my work was now going as badly as his own once had.

I am too cowed to provoke further cruelty.

16 September

Things can't go on like this.
And yet the remedy is worse.
Worse than this torment of fear and waiting?
Yes, since *loss* is what I fear, and loneliness.
How can I leave without him?
Such sweetness to remember his arms around me.
His comforting whisper.
Even if I don't believe the comfort.
Do people recover from such pain, or are
they damaged forever?

17 September

A hot night. Impossible to sleep. Hans is not usually out so late without phoning.

The rehearsal must have ended long ago. Even if he went on talking with the keener actors. Why do I go on sitting here? It is because I am afraid to go to sleep, and wake alone. . . .

18 September

Today I lectured at the Sorbonne on Niels Bohr. I have barely slept, and must look like a gargoyle. I was not sure I could even face so many unfamiliar faces; to move from a chair takes more energy and will than I can muster. And yet, the lecture was an amazing success. The taste of the applause lifted me for a moment, like alcohol; and yet, stupid and pointless as I know it to be, I could not linger. I dashed away from my friends to catch the Metro back to Hans. So he should not feel alone?

He has no such worries about me.

Or is it, as his eyebrows suggest, to make sure he is at home? I am ashamed of my own obsession.

21 September

I have lab space now, following a letter from Brandt (who is in New York). It does not much hearten me. Hans and I are moved further apart as soon as I begin to work.

It is strange how our situations have changed. Once, he seemed only to be interested in squeezing some *pleasure* out of life: in consuming theatres, galleries, books, lively people. And now, suddenly, all that has become frippery, and all that counts for him is his writing.

And I, who once grudged the time to accompany him into the cafés he loved, and the galleries he enjoyed so much more than I did; I, who thought all these years that the true centre of my life was work, can barely face the task of lifting a pencil. I force myself to go into the laboratory; but I am only pretending. No one is deceived except Hans. I know now that, all the time, I was in some sense working for *him*. To impress him? Not precisely, though perhaps I had once hoped for that. But yes, in some sense to have him admire me. It was *his* admiration I craved; and I do not know if I can bear life without it.

27 September

He will not let me question him. He will not let me react naturally in any way. I have to swallow my fear and my rage or else he will not come home at all. I know that in some womanly piece of myself from my adolescence. I made one attempt to explain the severity of that demand.

But as soon as he began to feel the blackness and bitterness rise in me, he moved towards the door. Hans, what am I to do with my rage if you won't let me speak it out? It will kill me. I shall be the one that dies, not you, you old hypochondriac. He paused only to ask whether I had made any further inquiries about visas.

– How many visas?

– Three. Naturally.

I had indeed begun to make inquiries, but the impudence of using me to find a visa for Hilde choked me.

– It is still possible, of course, in theory, but we should not count on it. In any case, it will be too late for me, I could not help adding bitterly.

– So you mean – if I can't love you enough, then you won't help me? he asked directly.

I hesitated: It's hard.

– Then I won't leave, he said simply.

– It is the crudest form of blackmail, I sobbed: I have tried to trust you.

1 October

Last night I behaved shamefully. Without dignity. I deliberately came home early, and waited for Hans to leave. To see where he went. He had claimed to have met some marvellous new friend, a man called Walter Benjamin, whose ideas inspire him with a new sense of purpose. He said he was to meet him at a café. Little as I know we can afford it, I took a cab to follow his. And watched him sit down at a table (with Hilde, certainly, but also with another man). I was almost disappointed, as I dismissed the cab. Why? Did I want fresh evidence to convict him?

I watched the three of them. They were so animated and full of joy as they talked, I sat and watched them from my corner across the street, with tears pouring down my face.

When they all rose to shake hands in farewell, Hans and Hilde left together.

Thank God I had the self-restraint to go straight home, since, absolutely contrary to all my expectations, Hans returned only minutes after I did.

He was full of the talk he had been enjoying.

– Magical. A Marxist who is not a materialist. He has come to grips with all the horrors of our time. Even the horrors of Nazism. And he has a whole library of which I know nothing to help him. Imagine. He uses the Kabbalah. The work of an old theologian like Abulafia. He laughed at me when I drew back from my own Jewishness. I didn't even know there was a Jewish mystical tradition.

– And even if there is? I responded sharply.

– I understand you, he replied, mercifully: It was what I said myself. But the point is that this man knows Brecht. Writes about him knowledgeably. He has read everything. And yet. He has this other face, which makes me read my own differently.

– And your face, too. He kissed me.

I can only take in, that, for some reason, our lives are entwined closely as a result of that meeting. It is almost as if, a book-list, and a few holy names, and sacred texts, have led him to forgive me for my Jewish grandparents. Perhaps it will even lead him to forgive his own father, as one rotten apple fallen from a fine tree?

I can only thank God I followed him no further.

4 October

Hans loves me.

His lips are warm, and his tongue is in my mouth, and I am not dreaming. He calls me lovely, blesses me. I am radiant with happiness. Fearless.

5 October

In my relief, I spent this morning walking about the *Marais*. It was as if, only now, with the warmth of Hans' love once again around me, I could spare the attention to observe, among the bustle on the Rue des Rosiers, the stalls of fruit and shoes, the piles of fish, the pedlars from Kovno or Kiev who filled the pavements with a babble of energy. Even the shops in the walls seemed to bulge out into the streets. I must have been blind or asleep; today I woke to find myself in the heart of Asia.

And that is not all I have missed. There are strange archways, too, through which I stare at secret gardens and statues moulded with a baroque loveliness that reminds me of Vienna. I can see as much without pain. The tight clamps in which I have been living for so long seem to have released me. I flow out into the world about me now with avid curiosity. Museums do not usually excite me. (It was something which long came between Hans and I.) This morning, almost as if in celebration of our new-found closeness, I took a few tentative steps into the Musée Carnavalet, which had once been the house of Madame Sevigné. Hans must have once given me some account of her life, since I could not remember reading any of her books; and it was for a time an unexplained pang that pursued me among the splendours of her carved chairs and glittering clocks. Then I recalled the unthinking, monstrous passion she had felt for her daughter; and with that memory, a flicker of my own early morning dream. There had been some childhood glimpse of Frederick, with his arms out, calling for me, as I drove off resolutely to the laboratory. Did I cry then? I am crying now, as I think of it.

Frederick. My only son. Though I must remember, when I asked him about it, only six months later, he claimed to have no memory of my desertion. His impudent face opened into an uneven grin; the charm of it mocked me. His mockery and his confidence were alike precocious, and I loved them equally. Even now, I only have to close my eyes and his whole childish presence is there. Black eyes, solemn in their concentration upon some piece of balsa wood sculpture. Or black hair flowing in the wind as he climbed some dangerous peak to pose, his thin, precisely balanced body, as if defying us to fear for him. He was always an artist. An artist, or a pianist, or perhaps a chess player of genius. The school could not be sure.

As the memories crowd back upon me, I marvel again at the insanity of sending him so far away. Only my crazy terrors of these last months have kept out the longing for him; with the first release from that pain, another knowledge rushed in to take its place. Not exactly anxiety.

I think of him at six, at the piano, his feet too short to reach the pedals, playing Mozart, Beethoven, Chopin. How much I hoped from him, how much I took from his gaiety. His spirit was the gaiety of our house. And his courage. At six, he outfaced bullies with his nimble wits. My own cowardice made me plead with him to placate rather than tease. But it is not his nature. He reminds me of my own father, who never bent his head to anyone in his life. Yet Frederick is so much more frail. My father was built like an ox; and Frederick is delicate boned. His wrists are thin. When he came back bruised from fighting, my heart was squeezed with a sense of his fragility. It is part of his beauty, which seems to spring neither from Hans nor myself. And yet there is nothing feminine in his carriage. He holds himself bravely. Like a matador, I often thought; prepared to take on the whole world with a sweep of his cloak. And by the same token, he was much the most fastidious of any of his class in his choice of clothes. Taking him to a tailor was an ordeal; where Hans could not have been more casual in his choice of clothing.

Was our closeness unhealthy? At least, Hans was never excluded. How could he be, when so many of Frederick's chief joys were those he had given the boy? Hans could play the violin and sing; it was he who had taught Frederick to sight read. They spent hours in the music room together. And their affection for one another gave me pleasure.

And yet it is true I was more dependent on the boy than Hans was. Hans had another kind of magic in his life, the pleasure in his own creation which my own work in a laboratory could not give me. In any case, gaiety was his element; he lived in it. Perhaps his example gave Frederick the secret of inner joy. He understood how much I was dependent on other people always: colleagues in the laboratory, recognition, awareness of what contributions I had made. Both of my men seemed free of such obsessions. Just as neither of them seemed to need, as I did, to belong to a team.

If there were quarrels over the child, they were always on questions of order which concerned Hans. I suspect he saw discipline as a way of freeing the child from the inheritance of his own family. He meant so well; yet I could not help interposing myself between him and the boy; could not help trying to protect him, as I felt it. And yet Frederick himself made no objection. I know it enraged Hans; because it was an echo of the way his father had punished his mother. The worst he could imagine for himself was to become like that. And by my resistance I could tell I was in danger of putting him into that role. How long ago it seems. And my fatal mistake was my attempt to placate Hans by suborning Frederick's charm to offer him. Soon he became impatient with it, saw through it, and began to look for duplicity. Some mistake I must have made; for their love for one another soured on absurd arguments.

Hans began to worry that the child would waste his talents, for all his wonderful perkiness; always, and in everything else an optimist, this he was not prepared to leave to chance. And so we quarrelled. How it hurts me now to think that we could ever have quarrelled!

When we had the chance, the one chance, in the one and only life I have ever believed in, *why* did I deny Hans the decent ordinary home he demanded for his son?

For there is a sense in which I felt we were a little above such concerns. Our ambitions put us above them. And Hans, in particular, since I always saw him, as it were, in the vanguard of our family fame, even if my stubborn muscles provided the bedrock of our fortunes.

How is he now, our Frederick? I think of him. Tenderly at

ease with all animals. The appointed caretaker of all the potted plants that abounded in our house. Green-fingered, so that an avocado pip would sprout for him into a tree. Where is he now, and how does he remember our old voices over his childish head?

It is a long while since I have wept for anyone but myself. Now I weep to think of him, imagining him as an orphan, imagining his loneliness. Or perhaps even these tears are selfish, and what I dread most is his forgetfulness.

When Hans came in that evening I burst out: we have lost him. Frederick. We have given him away to strangers. And he watched me oddly.

– It was wisdom to send him away.
– You opposed it.
– You were right to persist.

And he took me warmly in his arms, and soothed away the fears in my heart.

6 October

The morning was so brilliantly blue and sunny that we decided to breakfast expensively at a small café at the corner of our street. I have never tasted such delicious coffee; never relished the melting of butter into croissant in the same way. And the trees astonished both of us simultaneously. I do not usually observe the changing of nature, except as Hans once teased me, through a microscope. Now it seems to me that Parisian trees are actually a different green from our old familiar Viennese varieties. Even their approaching autumn has only increased their loveliness.

– I always said you should read the poets, he smiled.
– But the books you put in my hands never spoke of trees, I protested: Verlaine, Mallarmé, Apollinaire, René Char. I only remember the names.
– But Char writes of vegetation. He is a lush poet.

— Well, my French is not good enough I suppose, I confessed, without anxiety.

— What hours such a confession would once have taken to force from you, he exclaimed.

I perceived myself on dangerous ground.

— Perhaps.

— Don't answer mechanically like that. It is a way of dismissing what I say.

My heart began to stir and beat heavily, and I bit my lip. When he saw as much, a recognition of what he was risking seemed to touch him also, and he leant forward to recover my hand with one of his.

— Frederick loved poetry, I continued bravely: You taught him to do so.

— Yes, he replied.

But I could see that the thought of Frederick no longer had the same power over him **as** it had yesterday.

Whereas I was much troubled by a nightmare I recognize now I have had before. Frederick has been caught stealing a musical box. It is one of those so charmingly made in Czechoslovakia or Hungary, where it is possible to watch the moving parts going around. It is familiar in some other way too; inlaid with mahogany or rosewood. I think it is perhaps something from my parents' home.

Why should Frederick steal such an object? For I can see that he is indeed responsible for the theft. There he is, in some American desert town, with the box behind his back, being threatened and still outfacing his questioners. His stance is belligerent and a little sulky. He is being threatened by unknown adults; police, not relations. Adults who keep asking my own question:

— Why? again and again.

He never admits the crime, and, at last, a man brings out a leather thonged whip with which he proposes to punish him.

63

My cry of horror wakes me, as I think it may have done before. As I try to explain the horror of the dream, and at the same time make sense of it (for after all it was to escape whipping, or worse, that we sent him far from the barbarities of Europe) I am not at first soothed as I expected. Instead, Hans reminds me of how often he had called my attention to the boy's dishonesty. Appalled at his insensitivity, I realize I am still inside the dream, that I have *not* woken up! Or *cannot* wake up. And when at last I do, I am bathed in a villainous sweat as though in the grip of a fever. Hans is still deep in his own sleep; and I snuggle gratefully against him, waiting for the full morning light to come round to our window, and wondering what my mind intends me to understand by such a vision.

8 October

This morning I woke feverish. Sweat pours down every limb, gathers in the hollow between my breasts and runs down my face. My breathing also is alarmingly shallow and fast; Hans says I must have an infection, but the sweating may have more to do with a lack of oxygen in my blood. In times of tension, my mother often presented the same symptoms. Hans teased me. He hoped I was not going to become like my mother, for whom he had no great liking.

For the first time it comes through to me clearly that I may easily die without ever seeing Frederick again. The thought is so overwhelmingly painful, that, even though I know it is the very worst thing for my condition, I abandon myself to great sobs of grief.

Self-pity. Self-indulgence. I know. And yet it is as if my body will not obey my will. Tears choke me. And my mind presents febrile visions of my son in different guises. He is nine. One foot up on a footstool, playing a lute and singing. Mischievous eyes denying the angelic perfection of his voice. Then he is running home through the snow, a bundle no larger than a small piece of hand luggage, muffled to his eyes. I watch him fall down in front of me, unable to catch him. I look into his clear eyes. He refuses to cry. His courage hurts me.

— What will become of Frederick if I die, I call out to Hans.

Hans says: Don't be silly. Lie calmly. I will call a doctor.

He is frowning. But I cannot tell why he is worried for me. I know my face is red and puffy with grief. But, usually, he takes my toughness for granted. Finds my hypochondria faintly irritating. Today, he seems to be taking my illness very seriously, and another little clutch of fear touches my heart.

I'm finished. I'm finished. I have been destroyed by everything that has happened.

As the terror rises, I can hardly breathe. My chest hurts too much even to speak. Only hot tears continue to trickle down my cheeks.

I shall never see Frederick again.

I know it.

About half an hour later, Hans returned with a doctor from the flat below, who is also a refugee from Vienna. He will take no money; and insists on giving me sulphonamides nevertheless, which must be very expensive. Then he sent Hans away so he could talk to me.

I burst into tears as I tried to tell him my fears.

He listened seriously. Then he began to talk about his own son. He and his wife know very little about what happened to him, since he was first dragged out of his class at the University of Heidelberg two years earlier.

They try to hope he may only be suffering privations in prison; and that his health is not altogether ruined. His eyes tell the true terror. He no longer believes his own son is alive.

Hans brought me up hot milk with some tang of alcohol in it. He is protective. Calming. He reassures me: the decision to send Frederick away was the only sensible choice we could have made. I let him say 'we', because it reduces my own sense of lonely guilt, even though we both remember well how the decision had been taken after many battles.

— My brave Inge, he says: you will recover. You must recover. I need you. Don't you know how much I need you?

The warmth of his words, the milk, and the pleasantly aniseed-flavoured liquor send me into a luxuriant, pleasant doze such as I cannot remember enjoying for months. Perhaps years. Whenever I wake, with a start, Hans is still there at my side. He has a small bedside lamp on, and he is reading.

Sleepily, I ask him: what is the book?

— A typescript. Of Walter Benjamin's.

So we pass the night.

By the morning, I was in normal health; though still bothered with phlegm in my lungs.

— How strong you are, Hans greets me.

I wanted to get out of bed, and help him make our rudimentary breakfast. But he would not hear of it. He is as tender to me as if I were a child myself. I wonder if he, too, is thinking of Frederick. When he brings me my pills and another hot drink, I study myself carefully in the glass. Lying against the pillows, and still a little weak, my face has lost some of its tension, and I can just catch the old fleeting resemblance. The same ambiguously flecked eyes, roughly curling hair. I once became used to the ease with which other parents recognized me as his mother. And though I had never particularly rejoiced in my face, the strength in my features was excellent in a boy. Without vanity I could see that what might be ponderous in me would be handsome in him.

Hans has gone out this afternoon. The pills have made me dozy, and I slept without anxiety. Before he had returned home, I was out of bed (for all his protests). My throat was free, my cough gone.

— You are trying to impress me, he accused, but I could tell he was only teasing.

We are happy, I discover, wonderingly.

9 October

As for my brief joy! This evening we went to an early party in the sunlight of Erlichman's patio. Iced champagne. Hans looks so young, so triumphant. Leaving, I say as much proudly; and he smiles, with just a touch of complacence 'So. Would you let me have an adventurous life?' Drily I reply: 'I wouldn't have any choice.'

He finds that a grudging response, and our mood of friendliness vanishes as if it had never been.

Tonight Hans dreamed that a man had damaged his penis, and he was afraid that it would not heal.

10 October

There is only one thing for it. We must meet. All of us. I cannot go on with this unexplained threat hanging over us. I asked Hans if the girl would come round to supper.

— I have a right to meet her.

— I cannot see what good can come of that, he replied.

— I want to understand her, I said.

And my real motives? I think I wanted to put Hans in a position where he could not say one set of things to me and another to her.

— You are precipitating a crisis, he groaned, as if guessing as much.

— No.

—How can it go well?

— She is the girl who found us this room, I know that much. And I think I met her once at Mass before we left Vienna: Won't you arrange it?

Reluctantly, he agreed.

12 *October*

I felt very confident I could handle the girl, and whatever threat she presented. It was only a matter of facing her with our true situation surely? All day Hans tried to dissuade me.

– I'm not sure this is a good idea. I don't *feel* it's going to go well.

– Why not?

There was a long pause.

– Are you afraid I'll get hysterical? I won't. I promise to be perfectly calm.

– Not exactly hysterical.

– What then?

– I don't fancy it. I think we should call it off.

I don't know why, but his reluctance made me all the more determined. I should be on my home territory. I could handle everything, I thought.

– What time is she coming?

– Please, he said: I want you to think about this. I can't see what good it can do.

A little bead of sweat began to form on my upper lip, and I wiped it away. I longed for a strong drink, to steady my hands. There are important things I don't know, I thought. Hans is saying as much.

– Don't say anything about me, will you? he asked: That will make her see me as feeble. Or finished.

– Of course not.

He too was pale and wet-skinned.

– You look very nervous, I said brightly.

– Well, darling, you must realize. At the beginning of a relationship. You say things. You don't always know where it is going. You won't talk *coarsely* about her? I should have to defend her then, wouldn't I?

14 October

She sat in my room, radiant with confidence.

— We have to rid ourselves of all these bourgeois ideas of property, she said: No one belongs to anyone, as if he were a thing.

Her face was broad, and flat-nosed; not exactly pretty, perhaps, but healthy-looking, and young.

— Here you are foreigners, refugees. Can you not smell the stink of defeat in France? It will need a Revolution to save her. A war might help. Might at least temper her energies. She might emerge from any nightmare strengthened.

— War means dying. Many people die. A whole generation, sometimes. How can you want war? Still less Civil War? Are you a Communist? I asked stupidly.

— I am proud to be so. That is how I know, the terrible, possessive love you feel for Hans will only stifle him. You must let him go free. Let him do what he likes. Relinquish your hold over him. His soul is dying in your hands.

— What about *my* soul? I demanded energetically: Why do I have to connive at anything that breaks *my* human spirit?

— If you loved him, you would want him to have anything that makes him happy.

— You are suggesting I accept you as a kind of official mistress? But isn't that exactly the self-indulgence the old France you mention stinks of?

— There *is* an altogether more important struggle, said Hans.

— We are only a part of it, the girl insisted. Of course, I don't know if I can make Hans any happier than he has been with you.

— Have you known one another long enough, even to wonder *that*? I asked crisply.

— A year.

— You were away, surely. Much of that year.

– There was hardly a day when we didn't speak. On the phone, at least.

My heart cringed with the pain.

– I see.

– Darling, you aren't saying enough? Hilde turned to Hans.

And Hans was smiling all the time, always that familiar sweet smile I loved so much, but given to her, the stranger: You see, there is more pain here than you imagine, Hilde. You must be gentle.

And even then, I did not really doubt his love, until I heard the soft voice he used to say goodbye to her. It was a family voice. They were close. I could no longer pretend.

15 October

Hans has begun work on a new play. He says it concerns the historical dimensions of Nature. I do not understand a word of it. He is taking it round to his typist tonight with a great deal of excitement.

– What excites you?

– The whole phantasmagoria of the nineteenth century.

Yes, I thought, the ghosts and the voices, those I can hear. The myths and the lies: I can put my roots down into that holy mud any time I want. Those who are dead and those who will die and those who will smell long after the New Europe is built over them.

– How can I look to you for strength? he muttered before leaving.

Strange how he loves the modern; as if this whole century has not delighted in exhuming prehistory. It is almost a deliberate regression, isn't it. To childhood.

20 October

A letter today from Frederick. It is cheerful, and I should have been made happier by it. But I could hear the distance in his voice. He is forgetting us, I thought. He is making his own life, and adjusting; soon he will not only behave like a little American boy he will feel like one, and even if we meet again soon he will look strangely at me, as if I were a peculiar foreigner.

The thought made me fall to the floor and weep. Hans found me there, but I didn't care. I didn't care about anything else but the distance between myself and my only son.

He watched me with surprise as well as horror.

— Inge. What is it?

— It is Frederick. I have made a mistake. I have made a mistake. I did not know it would break my heart, I wept.

— You? You are like steel, was all he said, turning on his heel.

From this, I gather something new has happened, but cannot guess what.

21 October

Hans has been telling me the news from Germany. He is nearly distraught. Why? The news is bad (looting and baiting, and extraordinary sadism) but his misery looks as if something closer to home is disturbing him. All Jews of Polish extraction have been deported over the Eastern border; and, as the Poles refuse them, they have to inhabit a no-man's land in sickening conditions. Perhaps this hurts him.

And yet. It is a terrible thing to say, but I have only ever seen him look so wild-eyed about disasters which involve himself. His stammer, which we had almost forgotten, returns as I try to question him.

29 October

Hans has just told me that Hilde has been asked to return to Moscow. She is uneasy about it, as well she might be. Both Hans and I know of loyal Communists who returned in 1937 and then disappeared without trace. Hans is afraid to suggest she stays on in Paris, however, since the arm of the NKVD is long enough to reach her, even there; and her disobedience would certainly provoke some disciplinary action.

My one fear is that Hans might decide to go with her. I suspect she has been pressing him to join her.

Much may be forgiven to those who bring converts.

5 November

7.00 a.m. Hilde has left for Moscow. Hans accompanied her as far as Le Havre, where she is taking the boat across the Baltic. Every minute today I have been afraid I should hear he has decided to leave with her. He has taken all our money. What will I do if he decides to throw his lot in with her completely?

1.00 a.m. Not so. Praise God. Hans has returned to Paris. But he looks at me with pink eyes filled with hatred, as if their separation in some measure is my fault.

I have a sense that I will be punished for being a factor in his decision to stay.

7 November

Something terrifying has happened. A seventeen-year-old boy, Herschel Grynszpan, who is at present living in Paris, has been driven out of his mind by the fate of his parents herded into a camp near Zbonszyn. He has shot and fatally wounded one of the Secretaries of the German Embassy, Ernst von Rath. The indignation in Paris has swelled to the most terrifying proportions. And it isn't only the French that are behaving disgracefully. The leaders of the Jewish Community here are themselves among the first to insist on his foreign origin.

10 November

The news has begun to come through of reprisals taken against Jews still living in Germany. I can hardly believe what is happening. It is like an apocalypse. Synagogues razed to the ground. Shops burnt. Thousands arrested. Hundreds killed.

We listen to the news together, alongside the sycophantic mouthings of our Western leaders.

– You see? I should have gone with her, says Hans.

I renew my attempts to contact my old friend Brandt to beg his help for a visa to the United States. But the pressure on that haven is by now so strong that they have put up barriers against us. It is very difficult to imagine them listening, even to Brandt, when one imagines how many important men in their midst have the direct ear of the President. And even people with the strongest protectors in the States are failing to get visas.

– I was a coward. I should have gone with her, said Hans before we went to sleep.

England should be easier, I think. But the walls are there too.

11 November

Hans said this evening: I had a drink at a café with that Walter Benjamin again. He spoke of Palestine. He has never done so before, with Hilde present. Zionism! It's pretty alien to me. And the Arabs are probably as dangerous as Europeans.

– Whatever makes you consider it? I asked the man.

– I can hardly stay alive on what I earn here, he said.

73

He is in such dire financial straits that I lent him a little of our money. In return, he offered me one of his death capsules, from which I turned in horror.

I listened to all this with attention. Perhaps Palestine is not such a bad idea? In Hans' dream there is no threat to France. Not even to Czechoslovakia. I remember the plebiscite we were promised in Austria that was called off at the last moment.

There are worse things than dying; we knew that too. And if, in Paris, you cannot hear the shouts of *Juda Verreck*; thousands of voices are waiting, as in Germany. The whole of Europe is contaminated with the same hatred.

Yesterday we had another letter from our son. It is difficult, but not yet impossible for us to join him. I long to do so. If I were close to him, I could even bear the terrible gap that is growing between Hans and myself.

22 November

Hans no longer believes Hilde is alive. Many loyal Communists who returned with her have been shot. I laughed at him.

– Who would go back to be shot? Clearly, she did not believe anything like that herself, or she would scarcely have returned.

– Those who don't obey orders can be shot here, he repeated quietly.

I was still incredulous.

– Is this what you had been protecting me from?

– In a way. She has been working with several intelligence services.

25 November

He has received his first letter from Moscow. His joy is open and unashamed.

Nothing has separated us more.

Part Four

HILDE DORF'S LETTERS TO HANS WENDLER

'The face of the "angel of history" is turned towards the past . . . but a storm is blowing from paradise . . . the pile of débris before him grows skywards'
   Walter Benjamin

MOSCOW: 1939

12 January

My love, I want you to know how well I am here. And *happy*. (Or would be if I did not long for you every moment of the day!) This city, with its frozen mountains of snow everywhere and the dull grey ice of its river, and the gutters – well, it *all* suits me! As if I were the Brunnhilde you liked to call me, and not just your poor little Hilde who misses you so much.

Don't worry for me. Above all, *don't* believe all the lies in the Western press. We have fresh garlic here. And lemons. And I never felt more healthy in my life. I have a good job. They found it for me right away. I work in the German section of one of the big State Publishing Houses here. Not translating yet; though I am working hard at my Russian. But even if I am only typing, it is amazing how interesting and different everything seems here. I had no idea Germany was producing such a fertile stream of healthy work.

Of course, I can't live near my work. Only very important party officials, or famous musicians, or writers, live there in special flats. I live right outside Moscow – almost in the forests – in a wooden house. It's like a fairy tale. And you need not worry I am cold. In the office, the radiators pour out heat.

I am even beginning to save money. It is easy here. Rents are so low, and heating so cheap. If you could *only* summon the courage to join me, I could even buy you a ticket.

You must know I never forget you, and never shall. Be *very* careful, my darling, you are watched, as you know. And not among friends.

All my love,
Hilde

February, 1939

My love. No word from you. Is it possible the French are so *mean* they stop all post to the Soviet Union? The stupid French pigs, as if I didn't know what you would be saying without paper and ink! All the same I look in my box every day hopefully. Do write!

My situation has changed a little. But for the *better*. One of the other girls who work in the Publishing House has a boy friend who is a member of the Writer's Union; and they have moved into a flat quite close to the Tretyakov Gallery. There is a room they don't need! So imagine my good fortune. She has asked me to move in with them.

So now I live in Moscow itself, and can walk along the river banks, and go to the Museums, and see the walls of the Kremlin for myself. There is nothing in the world to be afraid of here; if only I could persuade you to join me, I should be happier than at any other time in my life. You cannot think how people value writers here. If you came, you would be a *celebrity*! The other day I saw Pasternak walking along in his huge belted coat, and everyone nudged and pointed him out to me. Can you imagine that happening in the West? I know the rumours, but they are not true; I saw him myself walking along the riverside.

Won't you believe me and join your still lonely and always loving,

Hilde

April, 1939

Still no word from you, my love, and I am beginning to worry about you in that horrible capitalist prison. You cannot know how many Poles are flooding into Moscow at the moment. Many of them are Jews, and such things can be said freely here, did you know that, Hans? There is a whole section of this very Publishing House devoted to the translation of Soviet writers whose first language is Yiddish. I am told there is a great tradition in it; and that the Soviet Union is proud of them. What more different from the world I have left! Oh, have *done* with it, Hans, and join me here!

I *do* worry for you. Are you writing? I fear your silence may mean you are not. You *must* write poems Hans, it is your work. Every one has to work. And yours is to write plays and to make poems. Another trouble: your voice. Has that silly voice impediment returned now that you no longer have your Hilde to tease you and soothe you? Reassure me.

I know you love me; but this silence is terrible between us. Write many, many cards and letters just so that I know you are well. Or at least alive. And have not forgotten me altogether.

Hilde

30 April 1939

My love,
Sometimes strange things happen, don't they, unbelievably strange like the happenings in a dream, that mean something to one person and nothing at all to another. Perhaps one day we can meet and talk about what is happening.

But I have a horrible premonition that we shall not meet again. That something has already happened to you. Or *has* happened. Or will happen to me. Nonsense, I know. I try to shrug it off, but without a word from you, it is very hard. My friend has quarrelled with her boyfriend. And he has disappeared. She doesn't know what to make of it.

For God's sake write. You can't *know* what it is like to feel that Spring is coming and there are still so many miles between us.

A lot of things can happen. Please.

Don't forget me altogether.

Hilde

Moscow
2 May

Dearest, I have been alone all week in this huge flat. Perhaps it will seem absurd, but I regret so much moving into town from my fairy-tale hut in the forest. I try so hard to remember your face, and your smile. If only I can think of you clearly enough and hard enough and truly enough I am sure I shall be safe. I wish you were here to hold me!

One surprise. I met Kurt here in the street yesterday. Do you remember Kurt? I don't think you liked him very much. Perhaps you thought he might once have been my lover. As if any such thing in the past could matter once we were together. He has changed. Looks thin, and his jacket quite threadbare.

He has nowhere to live, and has been spending the last fortnight with a cousin who is unfriendly and suspicious. She hardly knows him, so I suppose it is understandable.

For old times' sake, I said he could move into the room that is now unoccupied; though I joked: It has an unlucky history.

He sees your photograph on my wall, but so far hasn't made any comment upon it, which I find tactful of him, don't you? In the circumstances.

But he is away a great deal, and the silence here still presses in on me.

Still no word from you, Hans.

Hilde

Part Five
SYDNEY
20 September 1983

'Death is not punishment but atonement'
   Walter Benjamin

— So what happened? asked Inge's grandson.

— To Hilde? She was arrested some time in early May on charges of spying for France. Sentenced to fifteen years' hard labour. Which she served in full. And survived, said Inge Wendler.

— But Hans? I have translated the poems, by the way. You should look and see if you approve.

— How can I know?

— Tell me what happened to Hans?

Inge sighed.

— That is a long story. And like all stories can be told many different ways. Sometimes I see it one way, sometimes another. Today I see it sadly. As if we came up together to a point in time where all our past miseries could have been eliminated and with a little more trust we *might*, just might, have avoided all the pain. Today it seems unnecessary, what happened. But sometimes it seems to follow with a kind of crooked logic. Inexorable.

— But the facts, the boy demanded impatiently.

— Facts. And you call yourself a historian? Very well. I will tell you how I see the story today.

When the letters stopped arriving from Hilde, I experienced an enormous relief. Even the outbreak of war could not prevent my optimism returning. I had no problems with the Nazi–Soviet pact. It was no more appalling to me than the English and French betrayal at Munich.

But I worried obsessively about Hans. It takes time for trust to return, and I never learnt to renew mine.

83

He was writing constantly. Secretly. I no longer knew where he went at night; if he returned late, I did not dare question where he had been. And, since, for all his efforts, he saw none of the work of this period published, he always returned painfully unhappy. There was no consolation I could offer, and my attempts at comfort often brought back an ugly stammering stream of abuse. Some days he hated me; perhaps because he imagined my heart was now at ease; while he continued to suffer.

My heart was not at ease. How could it be? It has never been at ease since. I could not understand his anger. And he never expressed guilt towards me.

In my mind, his sudden rages sprang from a resentment at his choice of me rather than Hilde. I hardly dared inquire into that. I know now it was altogether more complex; then I thought it was my apparent facility in returning to work which made him hate me. Yet how else should we have had the money to eat?

In that year that built up to the war we were already thought of as enemy aliens. Worse, as émigrés, probably hoping to push France into a war nobody else wanted. Why should France fight for the Jews? as many thought. Hans read Céline with his own flesh shrinking in horror; and once showed me a passage from *L'Ecole des Cadavres*, where Céline speaks of the French disappearing body and soul from the place like Gauls, if there was to be a new war.

When war came, naturally, the French police arrived the next morning at our room, and Hans was taken away to be interned.

I was left at liberty, one of the very few times I have found being a woman fortunate. It gave me a little time. In Hans' face I read his hopelessness. He was already resigned to death. He had not yet shaved; and when I pointed this out, they courteously enough refused him the chance to do so. To this day, I can see the white fuzz of hair coming up through his skin.

We kissed then as if we were saying goodbye; and my heart lurched with the love I felt for him. Desperately, I rushed about inquiring where he had been taken; upon what charge; and what French friends we had who could help establish that Hans was no Nazi.

When he was released, towards the end of October, I was afraid at the change in him! His arms made no response to my embrace; and there was no solidity to his lips under my kiss.

I had lost my own job in the interim, but it no longer seemed important. I knew in my bones that it was essential to leave Paris; Hans resisted me. He resisted passively. But his passivity won. Because if he would not come, there seemed no sense in leaving.

We were deeply in debt by the time the Germans crossed the Maginot line in June. All of us, poor creatures that we were, now owed even the cheapest cut of horse meat to the charity of our neighbours. And when it was clear that the German troops were flooding over the whole of France, we set out South with whatever we could find. Your grandfather had two briefcases; I had some sentimental treasures – your father's letters – my father's watch, and a wedding ring, which I supposed could be pawned in an extremity.

We set out on 10 June. And it looked as if all of France were making the same pilgrimage. People moved in every possible conveyance; mostly walking, with pitiful bundles clogging the roads. But there were carts, milk floats, horses, bicycles. And every so often we were shot at by wandering enemy planes.

All trains were impossible. We were at first lucky in sharing a stolen French car; bought with the sale of my father's fob watch, to a rogue dealer, who knew the car could not possibly take us more than a hundred miles.

– Merde, one of our friends exclaimed when the car finally gave out.

Hans, who had said so little for months, got out of the car

with the rest of us, and shook his head. It confirmed his worst fears. We were not intended to escape. We did not deserve to.

— We must find a place to hide, I insisted.

— You are stupid, he said: Who will hide us?

But we found our own barn, and lay there; in my case more frightened by the noise of dogs than any other sound. I have never trusted animals.

— You *still* loved him then? interrupted the boy listening to the story, as light faded through the windows.

Inge stared.

— Of course. He is the only man I ever loved, she replied: But I understand your question. So many months ago I had been forced to accept what was involved in loving him. It is possible to love passionately and not be blind. He was not so much cowardly as careful in his learning from his experience. His life had been ruined from the moment we left Vienna; the brief success with his play in Paris was a coincidence of that emigration. What future could there be for a German writer in France? And gradually I understood more. In his grief for Hilde, there was always an element of disappointed vanity; but it was a generous grief, also. He was utterly without calculation. Hilde made no offer of fidelity; and he could not have expected it from her. I see you still find the depth of the bond I felt for him puzzling. It is unfashionable, I suppose, in your generation, where people marry more than once, I know. But for me, it was a bond as close as the bonds of blood. Even though sometimes when I woke to share his thoughts, his first articulated sentences in weeks. I remember he said: Even at your best, Inge, yours was not a mind that encouraged intimacy.

Yes.

*

What are the intimacies of betrayal? Dependence? Hatred? Animal terror. And a sexuality that breaks some private taboo. These things exist like a raw pain in the gut. It is not a pain you grow out of. The wound remains unhealed.

– You left me lonely, he sighed: I've been a lonely man.

And I remembered those nights in Vienna and Paris. Alone, alert, and damned into my own insomnia. Waiting for him to return. And closed my eyes. Again. Listening for dogs.

Once again I heard his old offer of compromise: Why not accept a decent arrangement? And my reply?

– I will never condone something which would break my spirit.

But on other days he said: My own love, the whole relationship with that other girl was nothing but a dream; a lovely dream, certainly, but one that vanished under my eye. Or your own clear vision.

I remembered Hilde's own clear eyes.

It was then I realized, for the first time, that whatever poor Hans did, it had to wound someone.

During the night, I began to hear Hans' voice mumbling in my ear again. Some dream has unlocked his tongue, I sensed; but when I woke, finding our arms around one another and his lips against my forehead, I saw he had been lying awake for a long time, and that his eyes were alert.

A stone weight fell from me, as I listened.

– We need somewhere to stay. Food. Friends, and patience, Inge, he said.

And looking into his face he seemed as serene now as he had looked so close to madness in the last months. It made me obedient and attentive. His manhood had been restored him.

If you ask me why, I can only say that it is as if some human beings, who function timidly and awkwardly in the circumstances of ordinary life, work peculiarly well when the whole world is under the same stress. As the whole of

87

France fell into chaos, so Hans seemed to find again a God-given decisiveness. And is it so astonishing? Who better to have at one's side, when the machines fail, and the ordinary expectations of daily life with them, than someone who has never learnt to manipulate or depend on either? The man in the dream becomes a hero.

So it was. Gratefully, I put my affairs in his hands.

– The Germans may be as far south as the Pyrenees now, he murmured.

Such was indeed the rumour.

– But when there is Armistice who knows? We shall gain nothing by rushing like lemmings into the hands of the first new supporter of Pétain who wishes to claim us as his due.

Pétain had not yet taken office, so I listened without altogether understanding.

– The first thing is to discover where we are. And then, to look for a big town.

– Not a village?

– What should we do in a village? How could we conceal ourselves? What function could we perform that would not make us instantly obvious? Besides, in every country the peasantry are the last bastion of suspicion. And since you have learnt only as much French as you needed to move round a laboratory, lie here, my love, quietly, while I make some local inquiries.

– Who will you look for? I whispered.

– An unpatriotic school master, he smiled.

And so it was we pushed no further towards the Pyrenees in June, and were able when the Armistice terms were decided, to make our way by train through unoccupied France to Marseilles.

But, by 23 August, we had new enemies who knew more than I guessed. The Communists had been taught to collaborate with their former enemies. I was more shocked than Hans, whose instincts were also pacifist.

– In the ordinary way, it would be the most sensible tactic, he said, in a measured tone which at the same time declared our terrible separation from those who were around us.

We were separate because we were Jews and because we were foreigners.

– The resistance to the Germans will only come later. When the French discover what it is to be under a German heel.

He decided Marseilles was our best chance. Around the 'Vieux Port', where there were enough whores and criminals to pay for the police not to bother anyone. Hans took my gold ring, and a necklace, which he had brought himself (I had put it aside as a gift that carried too many memories) and he went off to deal with the pawnbroker himself. He brought us back more money than I had hoped.

I can see on your face that you wonder why I talk of days *more* painful than hiding in fear, and on the run. Well, I only tell you my feelings. With Hans at my side I felt as if my centre of balance had been restored to me. Such is the insanity of a love like mine. There were other terrors – yes, *we* knew of them. What were rumours in Marseilles, were realities for us. Leon Blum might expect to settle quietly in the South of France; but we knew what happened to those deported to the East. For the ordinary Frenchman, after the mad rush South was over, it was not at all clear that joining the Free French under de Gaulle was the obvious moral response. Aside from physical danger, emigration meant facing criminal charges, and could easily be seen as a shameful attempt at escape. And, the British made it almost impossible for many to support them, when they bombed the French fleet at Mers-El-Kebir.

All this we easily understood. Who could understand a complexity of loyalties more clearly than we could? Nevertheless, the passivity of the Vichy regime, which Pétain was to claim as a shield to keep France from becoming a ruin like Poland, was already an obvious lie. If, in Marseilles we saw no Germans, there was nevertheless little guile in the French support for Vichy. Not then.

And this, even though the Germans had sealed off the whole of the southern zone, not only physically, but even to the post. And Laval was known to have plans, quite independent of anything the Germans might demand, to clean up, as he liked to put it. We talked of all this every night in the cafés and brothels under the eye of querulous pimps. We had no doubt that ultimately we would have to bolt for it. If Hitler was a friend of Vichy, then we were on enemy territory. As if to prove as much, our landlord suddenly decided to double our rent.

It was September. I was the one he asked; and I replied weakly that I could not give him my answer until my husband returned. Hans said we had no choice. He had been trying, without much success to find a vehicle that would take us as far as the Spanish frontier. But we could not afford to leave at all if our last reserves were drained away. I remember I began to cry: I shall never see my son again. I shall never see Frederick again.

At length he said: We cannot buy a car. We shall have to borrow one or steal one. Trust me.

Just for a moment an old pang of suspicion and pain touched me. It must have touched him as well, for he put a hand to my face, and said: Poor Inge, I have destroyed you. Forgive me. It was never my intention. Believe that.

I believed him altogether.

He fixed it somehow. We never discussed how.

And then it was a question of waiting for the car.

It must be what damnation is like, such waiting. People deal with it in different ways. I sleep. I have an insatiable hunger, it seems, to hide in blackness. The pain comes, though, with the first moment of waking. Into knowledge. No, you experience the pain *first*. Then the knowledge crystallizes around the pain and deepens it.

And fear? It dries your mouth. Have you felt that kind of fear? That destroys saliva, freezes the blood in your wrists, and squeezes the muscle of the blood's entry to the heart.

Hans lay awake instead, and let his thoughts ramble round and about irrelevant pieces of the past. He kept the light on, with an open book in his hand. A poor light, naturally; so the print could hardly be made out. And he muttered at me old thoughts squashed together into each night, and become a single, interminable stream.

You ask what kind of thoughts? So many. So muddled. So different. A mix of resentment, and self-hatred. He would tell me: You try too hard to be rational. The world we live in does not fit your model.

And I would turn into my sleep conceding wanly, it is possible. Why should I be ashamed of working as a scientist? And then my words would annoy him.

— Possible. Possible. Can't you ever offer some comment? Don't you have any opinion of your own?

And I would plead weariness, endless and hopeless fatigue.

And all the time I tried to close myself away from them, his words still had the power to bite into my brain like acid. Of course I wanted the change in him; the new direction and purpose. As if his strength could cure all the uncertainties inside me that went deeper than our desperate situation. Sometimes I had to defend my whole way of life as something worthwhile to pass on.

— The greatness of the past? he would tease me and provoke me to tears.

— This rubbishy age, I once dared to reply: You realize this age is going to look shit to the people after us? They aren't going to envy us living in this age, I can tell you.

— So when was it good? he could always counter.

— Writers scrabbling after fame. Where are the fine minds of this age? The decent human endeavour? I demanded him to recognize it as science. But I knew he believed none of it. I envied him his new certainty.

Sometimes he seemed to speak out of the Vienna we had left and lost.

— Lonely. I feel lonely. I should have married someone who would share my world. Why weren't *you* lonely, living as we did? You never even *wanted* a life with people and fun. *Did* you? You wouldn't even feel deprived in prison. Isn't it peace you wanted? To get on with whatever you do? Isn't *that* your real life? What *is* real, I might have said. But you see, I didn't want to argue. I was afraid to break the tenuous link between us.

— *Praise*, that's what you live on, I once risked saying.

And he laughed, as he admitted some truth in it. And what did I need? Friendship, I thought. And love. *Your* love.

— And where do my *needs* come in? he wondered.

What horror, I thought. To be sipped at. Like a child suckling a mother. No. More like a vampire. Just to think the word made me feel bloodless, drained, fearful.

And sometimes it was inexplicably different. I would wake up happily, listening to a voice that was sweet and loving.

— My lovely. You rescued me, I see it all now. How kind you always were. I see the whole past differently.

Until I thought: I'm dreaming this.

— Thank you, I whispered all the same.

— Sleep, my lovely, he crooned.

The words went on spilling out. Good words. I didn't sleep, but lay there drawing them in like balm. And when at last I admitted so much to myself I let myself turn towards him.

When his voice whispered in my ears without bitterness, I remembered how he had once been a joyful spirit, wanting to share everything he took pleasure in; and how he's always liked so many things. The sea. Wild animals. The countryside. Everything he did with the same energy. Shopping. Frying sprats, outside a tent. Cooking chestnuts in the ashes of a country fire. Pulling the burning skins off with his strong hands.

Yes, he'd been tender once, I loved him for that. If he wasn't always tender now; if I remembered so much bitterness that had grown between us, that was something we had to share the guilt for. We were like a machine that had worked badly; faults didn't come into it, I thought. The question was only whether it had all been inevitable. Whether the change had been avoidable by either of us.

We set out from Marseilles by car, on 25 September, and passed through villages built of pale stone, rising from valleys rich with olive trees. Travelling by night at first. We were in a landscape charred by fires; and under the moonlight, the earth looked white and thirsty. We could already see what Hans called the sacred mountain of Canigou, a pyramid rising above the other mountains. It looked like stone. At one place, where we stopped for Hans to piss, it was a desert of pale grey stone everywhere, as if some volcanic eruption had shaped the place. When Hans came back to the car he showed me a piece of agate embedded in basalt. And he gave it to me. I still have it. I don't know if it is exactly out of superstition.

I confess I was hopeful. Spain was still neutral. There were many rumours. Franco, for all he had taken Hitler's support, had left his frontier open to France. I remember being told before we left Paris in a hushed whisper that Franco himself had a Jewish grandparent. But my fatigue was too grave to speak of anything. Hans, in contrast, was insomniac, and spent the night chattering away to the driver.

I remember Hans asked me: Do you believe in miracles now?

— I'll tell you what, I said; I think there can't have been

enough magic to go round, like everything else. And it has been used up. Now all the wise men find their little spells won't work anymore. They have to use bigger and bigger magic even to get rid of a wart, let alone anything major. So now we're all on our own.

– Physicist, he teased me gently.

The road through the Pyrenees was not only unfamiliar, it was much more circuitous than we had expected. Our car was not up to it. We had to travel the last miles on foot; and in my case, since I suffered from vertigo, on my hands and knees.

Hans was in much better shape than I was physically. He carried all our effects slung about his chest with a rope, and was still able to hold out a hand, when I needed to drag myself upwards.

The last few miles took twelve hours. I cannot remember a single word we exchanged. Now that we were on the move, Hans appeared to have lost all fear; but I was shaking with my own cowardice; I drew strength only from him. At one point, what looked like a short cut brought us up to a face of rock which seemed insurmountable. I was ready to give in, with exhaustion, and sat down in the path. But Hans had been an Alpine walker and climber in the old days; and the sheer face of the crag did not put him off. Unloading his bag, he made his own way up by handholds I could scarcely make out with my myopic vision. I was afraid for him, but as he reached the top, he waved back to cheer me.

Then he asked me to throw up the bags. I had to throw them twice before they went high enough. Then, patiently, he undid the straps, and the rope; and made them into something which I could hold on to as I made myself follow his directions blindly.

– There, he called: Over a bit! There!

I obeyed him with my eyes shut, sick to my stomach. But when I reached the top of that crag, I saw the path leading down to Port Bou.

Our papers were by no means in perfect order; we were officially without nationality. But most of those who set out for the border in a similar condition had been allowed to pass across it. It was said to be a decision left to individual frontier guards.

We arrived in Port Bou by the evening, to be told that the border had been closed the day before. Our particular frontier guard had no love for Jews, and enjoyed applying his duty strictly. Every passport was looked at carefully at the police station under his command. It was up to him to grant entry stamps.

Ahead of us were four women, begging and pleading without success. The man looked self-important, and impatient; not very likely to accept a bribe, even if we had enough money left to do so effectively. All of us were escorted to the local hotel. That was where we first heard that Walter Benjamin occupied a room in more or less the same conditions.

Hans was all for going up there and then to greet him. He had not seen him since his Paris days. Some premonitory dread, rather than any word of mine, kept him lingering in our own room, however. I thought I had seen him downstairs a little earlier; and perhaps I had.

We were all supposed to be under guard; but I do not think it was fear for himself that prevented Hans from going boldly to knock on Walter's door. It was more a kind of moral delicacy.

The next morning at seven the news of Benjamin's death filled the hotel. It was premature; though certainly Benjamin *was* dying. The rumours multiplied. It was apoplexy. It was this or that. It was any kind of thing that the tongue could give word to. But Hans and I knew at once he had *chosen* to die. He had always been prepared to do so. It was certain that he had no thought of involving anyone else; but, in fact, his action produced a shiver of horror in the whole village, and there was no question of any inquiry being made into our papers for the next twenty-four hours. Indeed, the matter of our entry into Spain had now fallen out of the hands of the border guard into those of the local Mayor, Judge and Priest.

The whisper that Walter Benjamin had taken his own life passed among those of us held in the hotel with consternation. Hans tried to reassure them again and again that Walter had often thought of death; that it was something he had prepared for, that he had struggled too long against poverty and hunger, and could not face the failure of his own energy.

But they could not help reading more into his choice. It spelled out the bleakness of our own chances. The Europe to which we might be forcibly returned rang with the cries of the damned. We began to exchange stories of tormented friends who would gladly have died to be spared the torture cells even now being prepared for us.

For the first time in my life, I reflected how easy it was to die; how much easier, at least, than to suffer great pain. Or worse, forced to watch damage inflicted on the body of someone you loved. I am not a brave woman. As we watched Benjamin's corpse being removed, under blankets, by the police, I was hypnotised by the logic of his decision. Hans, too, seemed to pale at the physical evidence of peace that the silent body offered beneath its covers.

It was in that pause, that Hans, whose resolution had never failed him along the road, began to have doubts about the wisdom not only of entering Spain but also of our further plan to go to Australia.

Of course, if we could have found any means to secure visas to America that *would* have been infinitely more cheering a prospect. Neither of us knew anyone in Australia, and whenever we looked at the continent on a map, it was so far from Europe that it was like taking a long farewell from everyone we loved. It seemed equally far from our son Frederick, who had moved to the East Coast.

– Don't think of it as permanent, I pleaded with him: After the war we can return.

– Who knows if we shall live to see the end?

– We shall not live even to see its first stages, unless we take what chance has given us.

I found my energy restored as his diminished. He had often remarked upon that phenomenon; and thought it denoted something sick in our relationship. As if I preferred him low and weak.

He said as much then, and a few other things there is no need to repeat now. I brushed them aside.

It was true that a few other inmates of the hotel had already decided to be returned to a detention camp at Figueras.

And we had so little money. How could he look at the open door of our prison and even consider returning into it? I reminded him what had happened to one of my uncles who had failed to leave Vienna in time. The Germans had tortured him with cigarette butts; pulled out his finger nails; then threw him outdoors in the snow without clothes so that he froze into the ground and died like a man of snow. Worse deaths had been reported.

– Not in France, he said cunningly.

– Not yet, I argued.

– And who is to say we will even reach Australia? Who is to say that Franco will not make a new arrangement with Hitler? They are allies, after all. France was at least at the beginning of the war *against* Germany. How could I wildly consider committing our lives to a government actually put in power by German armed strength?

– What is really worrying you? I asked.

It was not that his arguments failed to convince me. I was as much affected by Walter Benjamin's death as he had been. But it seemed to me that not to cross was part of the same temptation. I was not altogether free of it myself. I put this to him, and he shrugged.

97

– You saw the hatred in the Customs Official, he said: Suppose that is the true face of Spain?

– We don't know that, I said. The hysteria was mounting in my voice.

– Arendt is still in Marseilles.

It was true.

– I don't hear of her running to Spain.

– All this we knew before we set off, I cried.

– I am not sure we were wise to expose ourself to so much attention, he argued.

There on the frontier, at Port Bou itself, we had one of the longest and least hopeful arguments of our life together.

What was he truly afraid of? Was it the thought of exile? The silence that seemed to emanate from the red desert of a continent where we knew no names? I don't know.

– Go on ahead, he said.

I refused.

– There you are, he said.

– I will not leave you now, I said, my voice rising to a shout: How can you even think I would do so?

Inge paused in her narration. She looked at the face of her grandson, and its questioning.

– And that is not what happened. What happened is more difficult to explain than the simplicities of desertion.

Inge took a full glass of brandy before continuing to tell her story.

You must try and understand. In so many ways our disastrous trek across Europe had cost me more than it had cost Hans. A writer – and perhaps particularly a poet – needs only paper and ink. Some writers can memorize their own works, and hold them in their head, or give them to other friends to carry in their memory. A scientist is another matter altogether. To work on the run, in hiding, out of touch with current thought, and above all without a bench and equipment, in my case expensive equipment, is imposs- ible. I am not a mathematical physicist like so many of my generation. Of course mathematics is a tool; but I needed others too. Expensive tools. These I would find in Australia. I was sure of that.

But Hans was leaving behind, not only the world of his language (there would probably be a few German speakers in any country) but also his whole tradition, the stream in which his thoughts came together. Our interests were not the same. Was that part of his hesitation?

I didn't think so. I remembered his resolution in Mar- seilles; and his courage in the Pyrenees. Whatever held him back was something that he had not admitted to me.

I was a little light-headed myself, we had hardly eaten anything for the last two days. I felt dizzy and off-balance, as though my legs were almost floating as I walked. Looking at Hans I guessed he must be feeling similarly weak.

– Please. Wait here, I begged, knowing that he was cap- able of wandering off. Being lost. So that I would be forced to cross alone. My heart banged as I wondered what I *would* do if he disappeared. But I had absolutely no idea how I would find anything to eat. We had little enough money, and the only security I had were our boat tickets to Australia from Lisbon.

I came out into sunlight, which was unexpectedly fierce, so that my dizziness increased to the point where I was on the edge of hallucination. As I stared at faces in the street, they all reminded me of people I knew well, one from Vienna, another from Paris, another from Berlin. And yet, there they were in black peasant dress, and I knew as I came up to each, the resemblance would disappear.

And then I saw the back view of someone I remembered from Vienna as part of our old salon: a back view, not only familiar, but dressed in the shabby clothes appropriate to

99

our situation. An old suit, once well-cut, and now shiny.

– Uncle Fritz! I called out.

And the figure turned, and was not an illusion. He had never been an uncle I had particularly liked; but to find a member of my own family in such a desperate situation put all such memories out of my mind. And I prayed he too would forget his own disapproval of me.

We threw ourselves into one another's arms. And I have to confess that the childhood memories of his snuff and peppermint that still, inexplicably, clung to his coat almost brought tears to my eyes.

– Will you have a coffee with me? he asked simply.

I nodded.

– Do they have a café in this god-forsaken hole?

– Inside. In these parts they get out of the sun. And of course, it is not a café in our sense, poor child. But yes, there is a village bar. Perhaps you would prefer a cognac?

– I have no money, I confessed abruptly. It suddenly occurred to me that his enthusiasm, like mine, might arise from his own need.

– I have a little, he reassured me: Where is your husband?

– In the hotel. He is not well.

He seemed surprised to hear we were together.

– Rumour had it that you went your separate ways long ago. Didn't he follow his mistress to Moscow?

– Do not let's speak of that, I begged him.

Inside the bar, the darkness blinded me for a moment; and then I saw all around us alien, seamed, dark-skinned villagers. Some were drinking at barstools; others taking food at the uncovered tables.

– Are you hungry? my uncle asked, as he followed my gaze.

– Very. But I am worried about Hans.

I bit my lips. What worried me, though I could hardly say as much to a man already reading my face with pity, was that Hans might not after all be still in his room. If I stayed long enough to eat the food that was being offered me, I might miss the chance to keep him with me.

My uncle shook his head, in a commiseration that I felt was insulting.

— Don't be sorry for me, I said hotly: Hans has usually been a good husband. I don't recall your own marriage, but I can hardly believe you have lived blamelessly. For me all that counts is our closeness *now*. And without him, we should never have reached Port Bou.

— Inge. Inge, he sighed: You carried him all your life like a stone.

— That's not true, I said angrily.

— A poet. What kind of work is that?

— Let's not argue, I said, suddenly enfeebled.

And I let him buy me a bowl of soup. But all the time I sat there my legs ached to be moving. To be running back to the hotel. To be checking up on him, I suppose. What other way was there of putting it? My uncle had activated old fears with the true ones. What if? I found my brain thinking. What if this strange hesitation of his *is* in some way connected to his old love? What if some message has been smuggled to him? Out of my sight. I can't be vigilant every moment. Perhaps even now while I try my utmost to help him, he is off to some prearranged meeting place?

— If such a thing had ever happened to me I would never forgive it, said my uncle, spooning food into his own mouth and watching me closely.

I felt my stomach clench, hungry as I was, against the good soup in front of me. All my hunger had gone. It was as much as I could do to pretend to be eating, still less allow the food to enter my mouth. I was faint and sick. It was as if, with his words, an old poison had entered my blood stream.

— I should never trust any such person again, my Uncle concluded.

— Trust? I tried to smile: That's a big word, Uncle. For a few moments out of one another's sight.

– Eat your soup, he advised me.

He was like a devil, noticing my weakness. There had always been something sadistic in him, I remembered. A Prussian uncle. What was he doing in Port Bou?

I asked as much.

He gave a melancholy smile.

– Tainted, like the rest of you. As it turned out.

My hands began to tremble, and I could feel moisture in my palms and beginning to form at my hairline.

– You don't look well, he said.

– Listen, I said thickly: What can I take back to the hotel? A few slices of salami perhaps, and a hunk of bread?

– You are agitated, he said.

– Yes. These times agitate us all, I said.

– Your crossing is arranged?

I did not reply to that, and he waved a waiter towards us. He could buy me the salami and bread I had asked for. But all the time he eyed me quizzically, as if he guessed my panic, and its cause, and felt contempt for anyone who could behave so submissively.

– I have never understood why people praise the love between men and women, he remarked as the package was put into my hands.

The strong garlic wafted to my nose, but did not touch me to hunger. On the contrary, it increased my panicky perspiration so that I had to ask my uncle for a handkerchief to dab my face and the palms of my hands.

– You worry too much, he commented.

– The heat, I tried to explain.

But really, I could hardly believe I had not imagined him, this Uncle from my past. In his presence I felt like a child again, suspected of all kinds of heresies because of my interest in science. I had to get out of his presence. I was in an agony to be at Hans' side.

– I have no money for any of this, I therefore explained abruptly.

– My pleasure, he bowed.

When I got back to the hotel I asked three times, in broken French, whether M. Wendler was still in his room. I could get no sense out of the man who had control of the keys. With something like terror, I then observed that the key to our room had gone. What could that mean? Was there a pass key? It will give you some idea of my state of unreasoning terror if I tell you that it was only as I put my hand in my pocket to find a pen that I realized that I had taken the key out with me.

A feeling of intense, if temporary sensation of relief flooded my veins.

Hans was in his room, but I could see at once that my anxiety was not altogether unfounded. Something had happened, something had happened. He too was afraid; and his face was wet with fear. I sat at his bed, and mopped at his forehead with my Uncle's handkerchief which I had carelessly taken from him.

– What is it? Has someone called? Have there been any messages?

He shook his head helplessly, as if he had no reply to any of my questions.

– K–k–k– he began.

And my blood froze.

He had never been affected with so severe a stammer in my presence alone. I could not make out what the word was he was trying to say.

– Can't? Captain? I guessed.

He shook his head again, and motioned for me to find him a pen and paper.

When I did so, he wrote in sprawling letters very clearly.

– KURT.

At first the name meant nothing to me. Then I remembered he had been a young student who had attended Hans' classes in Vienna.

A wave of superstition flooded me, as I suddenly

remembered his connection with Hilde.

But surely Kurt was in Moscow, or had been a year ago?

— Do you mean you have *seen* him? I asked.

He nodded.

— It's impossible, what would he be doing in Port Bou?

With horror, I wondered if he had come only to look for Hans.

— This heat, this town, it breeds phantoms of our past, I said.

How could I make him explain? He put the pen and paper aside as if he had no more to say.

Mutely, I offered him the sandwich. He did not seem to be affected with my own anorexic revulsion. On the contrary, he wolfed it down eagerly and gratefully.

Meanwhile, as I wracked my brains for ways, if not to persuade, then to kidnap him into leaving this accursed village I felt his head.

— You are running a temperature I declared. I will bring you some Vichy water and you can take a pill for it. I had in mind to give him two of my sleeping tablets. It occurred to me that with a little ingenuity, I could arrange a wheelchair and take him forcibly across the border as if he were unconscious.

— No, he said.

It was the first clear word he had uttered. Surely he could not imagine I would try to poison him?

I left the room with the door open, and hurried downstairs. I was afraid of the tap water, as all our generation were, no doubt correctly. All the while I waited for him to return I thought to myself: he always distrusted Kurt; Kurt destroyed him; surely he cannot have forgotten how Kurt behaved? And underneath all that was the fear: what if he is an emissary? If he comes from Hilde, how will he not respond as if his sanity has been restored to him, will he not recover from this terrible tranced condition?

What is he planning, what?

When I returned with my fizzy water, and my pills, the room was empty. Empty.

Can you not imagine how I scoured the village. Where could he be, unless some car had been waiting for him, how far could he have gone, and why?

I had one moment's hope when I thought he might have gone to the cemetery, to pay homage to his friend Walter Benjamin in his grave. The cemetery faces a small bay high over the sea. It is laid out in terraces, carved in stone, as if into the mountains themselves. It was as fantastic a place as any of the events and the people who had pursued us to its reaches. But there was no sign of Hans there. No message for me at the police station. No memory in anyone's mind of him leaving his room. Or of walking along a street. Or of getting into the car.

What to do?

You see, I could not leave without him. It was a terrible trap. That was something I could hardly forgive him for, that he knew I would be locked in the trap of that loyalty, that it might cost me my life, and yet he had left without a word.

You might say it was unlike him. Because in his own way he was a good and loyal man. And, thinking that, I stayed on, waiting and longing without hope. When I forced myself out, into the streets, I must have seen the half-remembered figure of Kurt many times; imagined him under a hundred disguises. Each one I approached, with tentative recognition, returned my desperate, searching gaze with a smile that showed the bad teeth of the very poor. Nowhere did I see anyone who looked like Hans.

Most of the time I sat in my hotel room, weeping. Sometimes it is impossible not to weep. The dignity we try to preserve is of little moment beside the greater blows of life. I have never met anyone who has been sustained by it; even in the camps, those who had most self-respect were often the first to collapse. I had collapsed easily before; but this was

105

worse than any pain I had known before. A nameless, plum-shaped pain that stuck in my throat.

Not the worst pain, though. You weep first, without understanding; and sometimes it is premonitory of worse than you expect.

The police brought a body to my room. They said it was Hans.

The clothes were his, certainly. But the face was shattered. Only his hands were unmistakable. His warm, soft hands. Loving hands. To my knowledge Hans had no gun. I understood nothing. And the police had no further information. He had been found in the main street; the very street I had run up and down in my agony of wondering what had become of him. No one had heard a shot or seen the accident.

If it was Kurt who had been deputed by some unimaginable agency to have him killed, then why? I felt only the pain. It is not a pain from which I have ever recovered. Though, as you see, I continue to live.

Sometimes I wake in the night, wondering was it really Hans' body I was shown? Could he be still alive in Europe? Wandering. Lost. And thinking I had abandoned him? It is all nonsense, of course. And yet, men like him managed, somehow, to survive German occupation.

Kurt was picked up a few days after Hans was buried. And then he was interned as a foreigner. Nothing worse, since at the time Russians, as allies of the Germans, were not harassed severely. Communism was another matter. But in those days many people escaped from French camps. Englishmen returned home with their wives, I understand. German nationals, who had acquired other passports by marriage, found it equally easy. I remember in Lisbon everyone who came through for several days was, by repute, Egyptian.

Kurt made no attempt to escape. He simply sat around and scribbled all day long. Mostly letters, I understand. He must have become altogether mad. He wrote many letters to his mother in Vienna; and she was already dead, poor soul. Dead, and known to her son to be so. They might have offered some clue. About *why*.

Or even if? Perhaps I had invented a link between Kurt's presence and Hans' death. Even now I am bewildered what to think.

Perhaps I was most bewildered because I learnt to see Hans as he saw himself. The sickness of his own self-hatred infected me. That hidden sickness was less easy to recognize than a mysterious stammer that came and went.

My blindness was something to do with the weight I gave our two disciplines. As I saw it, there was something altogether nobler in the activity of science. And so I suppose I felt entitled to a measure of approval, which I failed to accord him. I was not so far away from my uncle as I should like to have been. I thought of myself as a good scientist; regarded with more interest than I deserved, perhaps, because I was a woman in a field where men were accustomed to strive alone.

What friend was it suggested that *envy* lay behind Kurt's actions? Sexual jealousy I might have considered myself. Perhaps that was what Hans had in mind when he first discovered himself alone with his killer. But Kurt was not more than casually interested in Hilde. He enjoyed an easy success with women.

But what could Kurt envy in Hans? What else, but his gift. For language, the written language, and the poetry of his youth.

I don't understand even now. I feel as if all my life I have been part of an unequal duel, one in which I cried out in terror long before being beaten. I have always been defeated, not in one duel but in many.

In the massacres around us, one man's death counts little with God. What is important must be living out your own life, not someone else's. My own failure weighs all the more heavily upon me.

For this failure to understand I am in need, for ever, of Hans' pardon, and can never win it now he is dead.

– And so, my beautiful grandson, we should drink a toast to Hans' spirit. Did you know, this evening ends the Jewish Day of Atonement? Let us drink. To the forgiveness of all our infidelities!

Part Six

HANS WENDLER'S
POEMS IN EXILE

1

After Europe, Dido, all winter
the days rushed through me
as if I were dead, the
brown sea pouring into the cities
at night, the rain-smell of fish,

and when you ask for my story, how
we came to be blown along your
dock-streets, pocked and scuffed,
I see only my mother laced in silk,
myopic, her small feet picking over rubble.

How to make you imagine
our squares and streets, the glass
like falls of water, the gold-leaf
in the opera houses. There were
summer birds golden as weeds,

the scent of coffee and halva
rising from marble tables,
and on dark afternoons
the trams grinding on wet rails
round the corners of plaster palaces

such a babble of Empire
now extinguished, we can
never go home, Dido,
only ghosts remain
to know that we exist.

2

Unrepentant, treacherous, lecherous
   we loved beauty, in the tenderness
of violins, or the gentle voice of a girl,
   but we built over the stink of our dead,
our rivers ran yellow with the forgotten,
   Dido: the cruel cannot be blessed.

The endless sunshine, frangipani, gulls calling:
   How can you ease my pain or give me rest?
I had so little strength, had to believe
   my own voice would return
and win me power,
   no village kingdom satisfies that hunger.
In any case, the cruel cannot be blessed.

Things come too late to save.
   On the last boat, we'll sing
old prayers, and some will dream of quiet,
   but the sea will have most of us.
I am not prepared for white soot, cold ash,
   or the red sands of Australia. Forget me,
Dido: The cruel cannot be blessed.

3

Last night, my sad Creusa, quietly
   crept into my dream. As if
dry leaves could speak, she whispered,
   but I could not catch her words,
Dido, and I was afraid

of what had wakened her.
   She was a loyal wife, in times
when nothing was forbidden
   no pleasure thought too gross:
and contrition as poor-spirited as cowardice.

Shall I spread that disease
   over the known world in a single colour?
Dido, I swear it was Venus' weather in the cave
   the day our mouths first opened to each other,
sweetness in our veins, was innocent.

Monsters and blood I dream of now,
   and a long voyage, lost,
although the wind has filled our sails.
   I must not falter in my mission,
Dido, at whatever cost.